Edward Bulwer Lytton

The Rightful Heir

A Drama

Edward Bulwer Lytton

The Rightful Heir
A Drama

ISBN/EAN: 9783337343491

Printed in Europe, USA, Canada, Australia, Japan

Cover: Foto ©Andreas Hilbeck / pixelio.de

More available books at **www.hansebooks.com**

THE RIGHTFUL HEIR.

A Drama,

IN FIVE ACTS.

Suggested by M. Alex. Dumas' "Le Capitaine Paul" (Paul Jones, the Son of the Sea), and re-written from the Author's "Sea Captain."]

By LORD LYTTON,

(SIR EDWARD LYTTON BULWER.)

uthor of "*Richelieu,*" "*Lady of Lyons,*" "*Money,*" *etc., etc.*

AS FIRST PERFORMED AT THE LYCEUM THEATRE, LONDON, UNDER THE MANAGEMENT OF MR. E. T. SMITH, SATURDAY, OCT. 3, 1868.

TO WHICH IS ADDED

A DESCRIPTION OF THE COSTUMES—CAST OF THE CHARACTERS—ENTRANCES AND EXITS—RELATIVE POSITIONS OF THE PERFORMERS ON THE STAGE, AND THE WHOLE OF THE STAGE BUSINESS.

NEW YORK:
ROBERT M. DE WITT, PUBLISHER,
NO. 33 ROSE STREET.

TO ALL FRIENDS AND KINSFOLK

IN

THE AMERICAN COMMONWEALTH,

THIS DRAMA IS DEDICATED,

WITH AFFECTION AND RESPECT.

London, Sept. 28, 1868.

PREFACE.

MANY years ago this Drama was re-written from an earlier play by the same Author, called "The Sea Captain," the first idea of which was suggested by a striking situation in a novel by M. A. Dumas (*Le Capitaine Paul*). The Author withdrew "The Sea Captain" from the stage (and even from printed publication), while it had not lost such degree of favor as the admirable acting of Mr. Macready chiefly contributed to obtain for it · intending to replace it before the public with some important changes in the histrionic cast, and certain slight alterations in the conduct of the story. But the alterations once commenced, became so extensive in character, diction and even in revision of plot, that a new play gradually rose from the foundations of the old one. The task thus undertaken, being delayed by other demands upon time and thought, was scarcely completed when Mr. Macready's retirement from his profession suspended the Author's literary connection with the stage, and "The Rightful Heir" has remained in tranquil seclusion till this year, when he submits his appeal to the proper tribunal; sure, that if he fail of a favorable hearing, it will not be the fault of the friends who take part in his cause and act in his behalf.

London, Sept. 28, 1868.

CAST OF CHARACTERS.

Lyceum Theatre,
London, Oct. 3, 1868.

Vyvyan (Captain of the Privateer Dreadnaught—Tragedy
    Lead) ....Mr. BANDMANN.
Sir Grey de Malpas (the Poor Cousin—Tragedy Lead).......Mr. HERMANN VEZIN.
Wrecklyffe (a Gentleman turned Pirate—Heavy)............Mr. LAWLOR.
Lord Beaufort (Lady Montreville's son—**Walking Gentleman** Mr. NEVILLE.
Falkner, }   { Mr. LIN RAYNE.
Harding, } (Vyvyan's Lieutenants—Juvenile Bus.).........{ Mr. ANDERSON.
Marsden (Seneschal—Old Man)..............................Mr. DAVID EVANS.
Alton (Village Priest—1st Old Man)........................Mr. BASIL POTTER.
Sub-Officer of the Dreadnaught (Utility)....................Mr. EVERARD.
Servant to Lady Montreville (Utility)......................Mr. W. TEMPLETON.
Lady Montreville (a Countess—Tragedy Lead).............Mrs. HERMANN VEZIN.
Eveline (her Ward—Juvenile Tragedy or **Walking Lady)**....Miss MILLY PALMER.

2

SCENERY.

ACT I.—SCENE.—Castle ruins in 4th grooves.

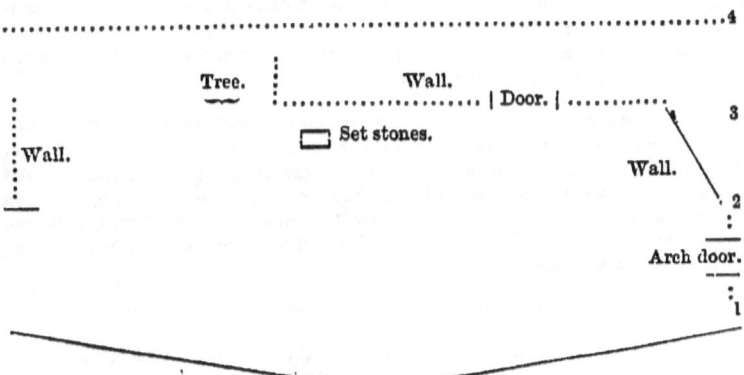

On flat, view of the sea; L. side, cliffs and castle; set wall, ruined, 10 to 12 feet high, along 3d grooves and L. 1 and 2 E.; open archway L. 1 E. set; low set wall R. 2 E.; a heap of set stones up C., to aid effect of picture; a set tree up R. C.; sky sinks and borders; curtain for covering the change of scene: dark velvet, heavily fringed and bordered deeply with gold, in two parts, to draw up and to each side; with coat of arms, royal English white lion and red griffin guarding shield and crown, in tapestry; over date in old English, 1588.

SCENE II.—Castle gardens in 5th grooves.

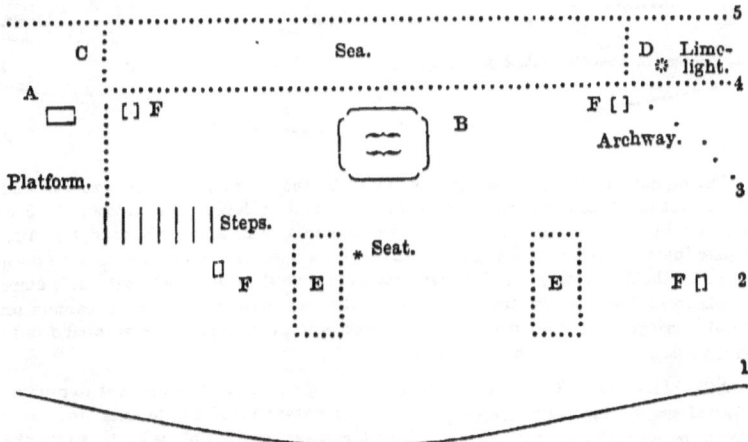

On flat foreground, dark blue sea, blending with the canvas down in U. E.; upper two-thirds light; bright sky; L. side, D., set wall of castle in U. E.; 3 E., set wall with open archway; 1st and 2d grooves wings, walls; all this side is dark; R. side c., set wall continuing the castle, supposed to be off R. 1 and 2 E.'s; the set end with a cliff, running down into the sea; R. 2 and 3 E., set platform, reached by broad steps, six feet above stage level; A, a box, with large box-wood tree, trimmed into fantastic shape in the fashion of the Elizabethan age; R. 2 groove wing, tree, run in to mask end of platform; B., a fountain, playing in an oval basin; in front of the basin, a half-ring of canvas down, covered with flowers and moss; E E, two canvases, covered with flowers, for flower-beds; a garden seat to R. 1; F, F, F, F, statues, three-quarter life size; the upper pair kneeling satyrs, the front pair nymphs erect; limelight L. U. E., lighting up R. side.

ACT II.—SCENE I.—Interior, in 1st grooves; Gothic architecture; R. on F., wide hearth, with earl's coronet and shield on the keystone; R. on F., portrait of man, half length, to resemble the personator of VYVYAN in face; the painting on flat makes the stage seem to be part of the chamber thereon represented; open R. and L.; table and three chairs on at c., table has blue cloth, corded with gold and trimmed with red fringe; chairs have an old English M, surmounted by a coronet, in dead gold, on the back, inside.

SCENE II.—Court-yard and Castle. Exterior, in 5th grooves.

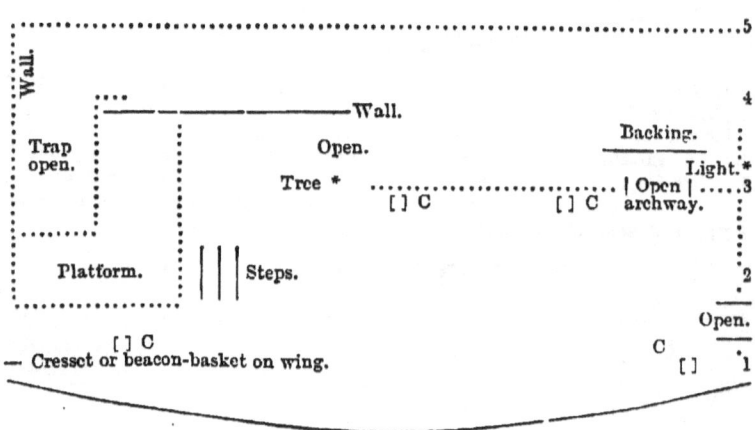

Sky on flat; the lower two-thirds is hidden by the set walls R. in 4th grooves, and in 3d grooves, c. to L.; L. side, 3 E., backing of wall, to large open archway in 3 g. set 1 and 2 E. closed in; small open archway in L. 1 E. set; dark, except L. 3 E., where there is a light; R. side 3 and 4 E., castle wall, ending in cliff over the sea; open trap, for the ditch, between platform (ten feet above stage level) and set wall; steps to platform 2 E.; wings are walls; sky sinks and borders; C, C, C, C, cannon on block carriages, the front pair pointed at each other, the upper pair pointed front; tree up R. of C., reaches to top of walls.

ACT III.—SCENE I.—Rocky landscape, sea and cliff, in 2d grooves; flat to roll up; view of sea, L. side; cliff running out over the water; all of 2 E. to sink and carry down the set rocks built up on it; along 1st grooves, low flat of rocks, to sink; sky sink and borders; trees and rocks for wings; sunset effect by limelight, L. U. E.

SCENE II.—Same as Act II., Scene II.; sunset effect L. U. E.; stage dark.

ACT IV.—SCENE I.—Same as Act II., Scene I.; table and chairs not on; a chair and a settee L.

SCENE II.—Cliff and Sea, in 4th grooves.

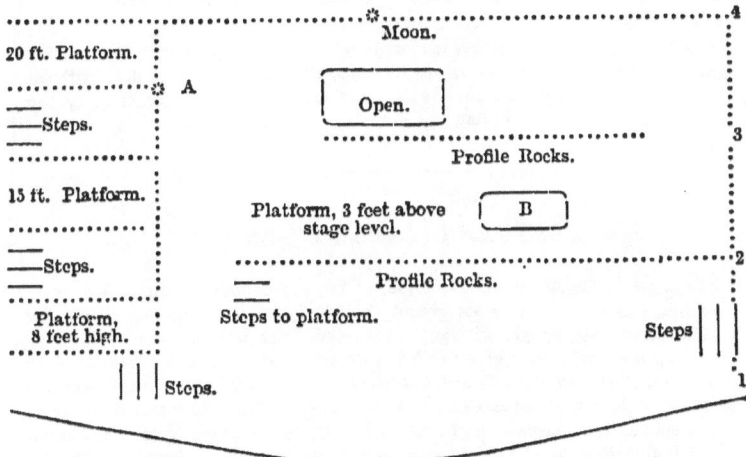

Limelight for moonlight, L. U. F.; sea on flat, with full moon at c.; the wing run in on 4th groove, R., is a profile edge of cliff; by having a piece stand out half way up its height, the piece will seem to be the base of another cliff, still further out in the sea; L. side, rocky cliff, covering in all; 1 E., set steps, leading from off down upon stage; sky wings, except L. 1 G., which is rocks; R. side, a series of rocks, forming steps and platforms; all practicable; A, a tree on the platform edge, joined to a piece facing the platform, so that, on VYVYAN seizing it, his weight brings it down, forces it to draw the piece joining it to L., and deposits him in open trap c., in 3 E.; B, a trap-net used in this scene.

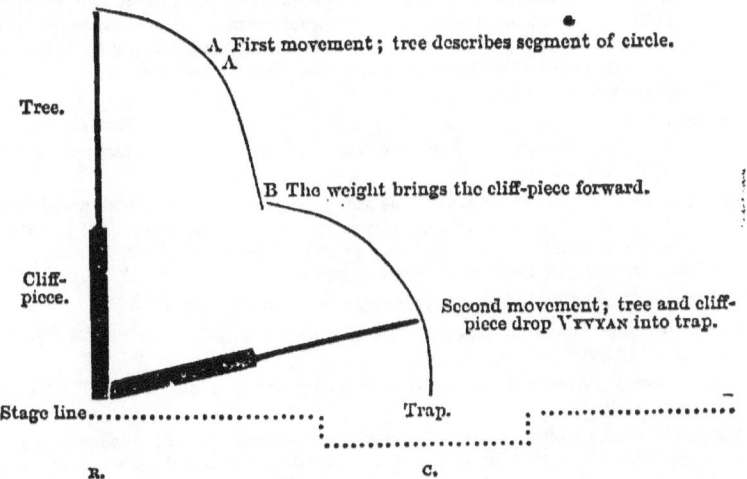

ACT V.—Scene I.—Same as Act IV., Scene II. ; Trap B (see Act IV., Scene II.) is open ; dark.

Scene II.—Interior, in 1st grooves ; deep sink, rafters and ceiling ; window R. C. in F. open ; two chairs.

Scene III.—Hall in 5th grooves ; closed in R. and L. ; upper E. gallery to bear weight of spectators ; large archway in its front, 4th grooves ; L. 2 E., dais, with canopy over ; royal arms behind chair ; table L. C. ; arch R. 3 E. ; bannerets hung from wall ; stained glass window in flat.

COSTUMES (*English, Elizabethan*).

Vyvyan.—*Act I.*: Black hard felt hat, four or five inches high in the crown, with a white ostrich feather ; steel gorget, polished ; three yards long scarlet sash, six inches wide, fringed with gold at the end, from left shoulder to right hip, tied behind, with loose ends ; buff leather jerkin, sleeveless : belt around waist ; rapier, black and steel sheath, cut steel hilt ; doublet and loose breeches of slate blue, striped up and down with black cord on the doublet, striped in *chevron* on the breeches ; buff boots pulled up to above the knee ; small satchel of buff leather, hung on right side, with dagger under it ; short curl black wig, rather short ; moustache and imperial ; make-up after pictures of Essex, Raleigh or Drake. *Act II.—Scene I.*: Gorget and jerkin removed. *Scene II.*: Red scarf ; sword like the other, in similar sheath, for throwing aside. *Act III. and IV.*: Same as last ; hat, no sword. *Act V.*: Half armor ; helmet, with vizor to close ; white plume ; blue sash ; steel-plated gauntlets, right hand one to be thrown on stage ; high russet boots ; thigh armor in plates.

Grey de Malpas.—Face made up for pale, cold, passionless expression, prematurely aged ; moustache and imperial. *Act I.*: Brown doublet, striped with yellow cord ; slate-colored tights ; shoes. *Scene II.*: Same ; fur cloak, with hanging sleeves ; flat cap ; cane. *Act V.*: Same as first dress ; cane.

Wrecklyffe.—Black wig, long loose hair ; moustache, with flowing ends ; chin beard ; scar across right eyebrow and cheekbone ; steel cap ; long, narrow mantle of dark glazed sea-green water-proof, worn carelessly over one arm and about the body ; short cutlass ; brace of brass-mounted pistols stuck in belt ; arms bare to the elbow ; seaman's sleeveless jacket worn loosely over a breast-plate, tarnished.

Godfrey Seymour.—Old man ; white wig and moustache : black velvet skull-cap ; red velvet doublet, with hanging sleeves, trimmed with gold lace ; slate-colored tights ; velvet shoes.

Beaufort.—*Act I.*: Handsome suit, blue and gold ; sword ; blue velvet round cap, with white plume ; russet boots drawn up to above the knee. *Act V.*: Red and black doublet ; red tights ; black velvet shoes ; long dark mantle, with sleeves, trimmed deeply with ermine ; face pale.

Falkner.—Plumed hat ; back and breast-plates · sword ; high boots.

Harding.—Like **Falkner**, with variation in color of his doublet sleeves, of feather of his hat, etc.

Alton.—Long white beard ; white wig ; dark cowl and long gown. *Act V.*: Skull-cap ; staff.

Mansden.—Long white hair, white moustache and chin beard ; handsome laced suit ; doublet ; trunk hose ; velvet shoes, slashed and puffed ; long white staff, with gilt coronet on top.

For Conclusion of costumes, etc, see pages. 47 and 48.

THE RIGHTFUL HEIR.

ACT I.

SCENE I.—*Castle Ruins in 4th grooves. Music.*

Discover SIR GREY, *digging, up* C., *throws down his spade and comes down* C

SIR GREY. I cannot dig. Fie, what a helpless thing
    Is the white hand of well-born poverty !
    And yet between this squalor and that pomp (*looks up* L.)
    Stand but two lives, a woman's and a boy's—
    But two frail lives. I may outlive them both. (R. C.)

Enter WRECKLYFFE, L. 1 E.

WRECK. Ay, that's the house—the same; the master changed,
    But less than I am. Winter creeps on him,
    Lightning hath stricken me. Good-day.
SIR G.   Pass on.
    No spendrift hospitable fool spreads here
    The board for strangers. Pass.
WRECK.   Have years so dimmed
    Eyes once so keen, De Malpas ?
SIR. G. (*after a pause*).   Ha ! Thy hand.
    What brings thee hither ?
WRECK.   " Brings me ? " say " hurled back."
    First, yellow pestilence, whose ghastly wings
    Guard, like the fabled griffin, India's gold ;
    Unequal battle next ; then wolfish famine ;
    And lastly storm (rough welcome to England)
    Swept decks from stern to stem; to shore was flung
    A lonely pirate on a battered hulk !
    One wreck rots stranded ;—you behold the other.
SIR G. Penury hath still it's crust and roof-tree—share them.
    Time has dealt hardly with us both, since first
    We two made friendship—thou straight-limbed, well-favored,
    Stern-hearted, disinherited dare-devil.
WRECK. And thou ?——
SIR G. (*smiles*).   A stroke paints me. My lord's poor cousin.
    How strong thou wert, yet I could twist and wind thee
    Round these slight hands ; that is the use of brains.

WRECK. Still jokes and stings ?

SIR. G.   Still a poor cousin's weapons.

WRECK. Boast brains, yet starve ?

SIR G.   Still a poor cousin s fate, sir.
   Pardon my brains, since oft' thy boasts they pardoned ;
   (Sad change since then). when rufflers aped thy swagger,
  'And village maidens sighed and, wondering, asked
   Why heaven made men so wicked—and so comely.

WRECK. (*gruffly*). 'Sdeath ! Wilt thou cease ?

SIR G.   That scar upon thy
   Front bespeaks grim service.

WRECK.   In thy cause, De Malpas ;
   The boy, whom at thine instance I allured
   On board my bark, left me this brand of Cain.

SIR G. That boy——

WRECK.   Is now a man, (SIR GREY *starts*) and on these shores,
   This morn I peered from yonder rocks that hid me,
   And saw his face. I whetted then this steel:
   Need'st thou his death ? In me behold Revenge !

SIR G. He lives—he lives ! There is a third between
   The beggar and the earldom.

WRECK. (*looks* R.).   Steps and voices ;
   When shall we meet alone ? Hush ! it is he.

SIR G. He with he plume ?

WRECK.   Ay.

SIR G.   Quick ; within.

WRECK.   And thou ɩ

SIR G. I dig the earth ; see the grave-digger's tool. (*goes up* R. C.)
                            [*Exit* WRECKYLFFE, D. *in* 8 G., *set flat.*

       Enter HARDING *and* SAILORS, R. 1 E.

HARD. Surely 'twas here the captain bade us meet him
   While he went forth for news ?

FIRST SAILOR.   He comes.

        Enter VYVYAN, R. 1 E.

HARD.   Well, captain.
  What tidings of the Spaniard's armament ?

VYV. Bad, for they say the fighting is put off,
   And storm in Biscay driven back the Dons.
   This is but rumor—we will learn the truth.
   Harding, take horse and bear these lines to Drake—(*gives paper*
   If yet our country needs stout hearts to guard her,
   He'll not forget the men on board the Dreadnaught.
   Thou canst be back ere sunset with his answer,
   And find me in yon towers of Montreville.
                    [*Exit* HARDING, R. 1 E.
   Meanwhile make merry in the hostel, lads,
   And drink me out these ducats in this toast :—(*gives coin*)
   " No foes be tall eno' to wade the moat
   Which girds the fort whose only walls are men."
              [SAILORS *cheer, and exeunt* R. 1 E.

VYV. (C.). I never hailed reprieve from war till now.
   Heaven grant but time to see mine Eveline,
   And learn my birth from Alton.

Enter FALKNER, L. 1 E.

FALK.   Captain. (*meets* VYVYAN, C.)
VYV.   Falkner!
So soon returned? Thy smile seems fresh from home.
All well there?
FALK.   Just in time to make all well.
My poor old father!—bailiffs at his door;
He tills another's land, and crops had failed.
I poured mine Indian gold into his lap,
And cried, " O father wilt thou now forgive
The son who went to sea against thy will?"
VYV. And he forgave.—Now tell me of thy mother;
I never knew one, but I love to mark
The quiver of a strong man's bearded lip
When his voice lingers on the name of mother.
Thy mother bless'd thee——
FALK.   Yes, I——(*falters and turns aside.*)
                 Pshaw! methought
Her joy was weeping on my breast again!
VYV. I envy thee those tears.
FALK.   Enough of me!
Now for thyself. What news? Thy fair betrothed—
The maid we rescued from the turband corsair
With her brave father in the Indian seas—
Found and still faithful?
VYV.   Faithful I will swear it;
But not yet found. Her sire is dead—the stranger
Sits at his hearth—and with her next of kin,
Hard by this spot—yea, in yon sunlit towers (*points up* L.)
Mine Eveline dwells.
FALK.   Thy foster father, Alton,
Hast thou seen him?
VYV.   Not yet. My Falkner, serve me.
His house is scarce a two hours' journey hence,
The nearest hamlet will afford a guide;
Seek him and break the news of my return,
Say I shall see him ere the day be sped.
And, hearken, friend (good men at home are apt
To judge us sailors harshly), tell him this—
On the far seas his foster son recalled
Prayers taught by age to childhood, and implored
Blessings on that gray head. Farewell! (FALKNER *exits* R. 1 E.)
    Now, Eveline.   [*Exit*, VYVYAN L. 1 E.
SIR G. (*comes down* L. C.). Thou seekest those towers—go! I will meet
    thee there.
He must not see the priest—the hour is come
Absolving Alton's vow to guard the secret;
Since the boy left, two 'scutcheons moulder o'er
The dust of tombs from which his rights ascend;
He must not see the priest—but how forestall him?—
Within! For there dwells Want, Wit's counsellor,
Harboring grim Force, which is Ambition's tool.
           [*Exit* SIR GREY, D *in* 3 G. *flat.*

Drop Curtain for change. Music during wait.

Scene changes to

SCENE II.—*Castle Gardens in 5th grooves.*

Enter, R. U. E., LADY MONTREVILLE, *by steps to* C.

LADY M. This were his birthday, were he living still!
But the wide ocean is his winding sheet,
And his grave—here! (*hand to heart*) I dreamed of him last
    night.
Peace! with the dead, died shame and glozing slander;
In the son left me still, I clasp a world
Of blossoming hopes which flower beneath my love,
And take frank beauty from the flattering day.
And——but my Clarence—in his princely smile
How the air brightens.

Enter LORD BEAUFORT *and* MARSDEN, L. 3 E.

LORD B. (*to* MARSDEN).   Yes, my gallant roan,
And stay—be sure the falcon, which my lord
Of Leicester sent me; we will try its metal. (*goes up* R. C.)
MARS. Your eyes do bless him, madam, so do mine:
A gracious spring; Heaven grant we see its summer!
Forgive, dear lady, your old servant's freedom.
LADY M. Who loves him best, with me ranks highest, Marsden.
                    [*Exit* MARSDEN, L. 2 E.
Clarence, you see me not.
LORD B. (*comes down*).   Dear mother, welcome. (R *of* LADY M.)
Why do I miss my soft-eyed cousin here?
LADY M. It doth not please me, son, that thou should'st haunt
Her steps, and witch with dulcet words her ear.
Eveline is fair, but not the mate for Beaufort.
LORD B. Mate! Awful word! Can youth not gaze on beauty
Save by the torch of Hymen? To be gallant,
Melt speech in sighs, or murder sense in sonnets,
Veer with each change in Fancy's April skies,
And o'er each sun-shower fling its fleeting rainbow.
All this——
LADY M. (*gloomily*). Alas, is love.
LORD B.   No! Love's light prologue,
The sportive opening to the serious drama;
The pastime practice of Dan Cupid's bow,
Against that solemn venture at the butts
At which fools make so many random shafts,
And rarely hit the white! Nay, smile, my mother;
How does this plume become me?
LADY M.   Foolish boy!
It sweeps too loosely.
LORD B.   Now-a-days, man's love
Is worn as loosely as I wear this plume—
A glancing feather stirred with every wind
Into new shadows o'er a giddy brain,
Such as your son's. Let the plume play, sweet mother.
LADY M. Would I could chide thee? (*to* R. C.)
LORD B. (*to* L.).   Hark, I hear my steed

Neighing impatience; and my falcon frets
Noon's lazy air with lively silver bells ;
Now, madam, look to it—no smile from me
When next we meet,—no kiss of filial duty,
Unless my fair-faced cousin stand beside you,
Blushing " Peccavi" for all former sins—
Shy looks, cold words, this last unnatural absence,
And taught how cousins should behave to cousins.
[Exit LORD BEAUFORT, L. 3 E.
LADY M. Trifler! And yet the faults that quicken fear
    Make us more fond—we parents love to pardon. (goes up C.)

Enter EVELINE, R. 1 E., weaving flowers—not seeing LADY MONTREVILLE.

EVEL. (sings).   Bud from the blossom,
            And leaf from the tree,
        Guess why in weaving
            I sing " Woe is me ! " (goes up C. to wall.)

        'Tis that I weave you
            To drift on the sea,
        And say, when ye find him,
            Who sang " Woe is me ! "
(casts garland over wall, blows a kiss, and comes down C.)

LADY M. A quaint but mournful rhyme.
EVEL.   You, madam!—pardon!
LADY M. What tells the song ?
EVEL.   A simple village tale
    Of a lost seaman, and a crazed girl,
    His plighted bride—good Marsden knew her well,
    And oft-times marked her singing on the beach,
    Then launch her flowers, and smile upon the sea.
    I know not why—both rhyme and tale do haunt me.
LADY M. Sad thoughts haunt not young hearts, thou senseless child.
EVEL. Is not the child an orphan ? (both at C., she R. of LADY M.)
LADY M.   In those eyes
    Is there no moisture softer than the tears
    Which mourn a father ? Roves thy glance for Beaufort ?
    Vain girl, beware! The flattery of the great
    Is but the eagle's swoop upon the dove,
    And, in descent, destroys.
EVEL.   Can you speak thus,
    Yet bid me grieve not that I am an orphan ?
[Exit, thoughtfully, L. 2 E.
LADY M. (aside). I have high dreams for Beaufort ; bright desires !
    Son of a race whose lives shine down on Time
    From lofty tombs, like beacon-towers o'er ocean,
    He stands amidst the darkness of my thought,
    Radiant as Hope in some lone captive's cell.
    Far from the gloom around, mine eyes, inspired,
    Pierce to the future, when these bones are dust,
    And see him loftiest of the lordly choirs
    Whose swords and coronals blaze around the throne,
    The guardian stars of the imperial isle—
    Kings shall revere his mother.
(seats herself in garden seat thoughtfully.)

Enter, R. 1 E., SIR GREY, *speaking to* SERVANT.

SIR G. What say'st thou?

SERVANT (*insolently*). Sir Grey—ha! ha!—Lord Beaufort carves your
    pardon,
    He shot your hound—its bark disturbed the deer.

SIR G. The only voice that welcomed me! A dog—
    Grudges he that? (R. C.)

SERVANT.   Oh, sir, 'twas done in kindness
    To you and him; the dog was wondrous lean, sir!

SIR G. I thank my lord!   [*Exit* SERVANT, R. 1 E., *laughing*.
    So my poor Tray is killed!
    And yet *that* dog but barked—can *this* not bite?
    (*approaches* LADY MONTREVILLE, *vindictively in a whisper*.)
    He lives!

LADY M.   He! who?

SIR G.   The heir of Montreville!
    Another, and an elder Beaufort, lives! (LADY M. *rises*.)
    (*Aside*.) So—the fang fixes fast—good—good! (L. C. *front*.)

LADY M.   ·Thou saidst
    Ten years ago—" Thy first-born is no more—
    Died in far seas."

SIR G.   So swore my false informant.
    But now, the deep that took the harmless boy
    Casts from its breast the bold-eyed daring man.

LADY M. Clarence! My poor proud Clarence! (C.)

SIR G. (L. C. *front*).   Ay, *poor* Clarence!
    True; since his father, by his former nuptials,
    Had other sons, if you, too, own an elder,
    Clarence is poor, as poor as his poor cousin.
    Ugh! but the air is keen, and Poverty
    Is thinly clad; subject to rheums and agues, (*shivers*)
    Asthma and phthisic, (*coughs*) pains in the loins and limbs,
    And leans upon a crutch, like your poor cousin.
    If Poverty begs. Law sets it in the stocks;
    If it is ill, the doctors mangle it;
    If it is dying, the priests scold at it;
    And, when 'tis dead, rich kinsmen cry, "Thank heaven!"
    Ah! If the elder prove his rights, dear lady,
    Your younger son will know what's poverty!

LADY M. Malignant, peace! why doest thou torture me?
    The priest who shares alone with us the secret
    Hath sworn to guard it.

SIR G.   Only while thy sire
    And second lord survived. Yet, what avails
    In law his tale, unbacked by thy confession?

LADY M. He hath proofs, clear proofs. Thrice woe to Clarence!

SIR G. Proofs—written proofs?

LADY M.   Of marriage, and the birth!

SIR G. Wherefore so long was this concealed from me?

LADY M. (*haughtily*). Thou wert my father's agent, Grey De Malpas,
    Not my familiar.

SIR G. (*proudly*).   Here, then, ends mine errand. (*going* L.)

LADY M. Stay, sir—forgive my rash and eager temper;
    Stay, stay, and counsel me. What! sullen still?
    Needest thou gold? befriend, and find me grateful.

Sir G. Lady of Montreville, I was once young,
 And pined for gold, to wed the maid I loved:
 Your father said, " Poor cousins should not marry,"
 And gave that sage advice in lieu of gold.
 A few years later, and I grew ambitious,
 And longed for wars and fame, and foolish honors:
 Then I lacked gold, to join the knights, mine equals,
 As might become a Malpas, and your kinsman:
 Your father said he had need of his poor cousin
 At home to be his huntsman, and his falconer!
Lady M. Forgetful! After my first fatal nuptials
 . And their sad fruit, count you as naught——
Sir G.   My hire!
 For service and for silence; not a gift.
Lady M. And spent in riot, waste, and wild debauch!
Sir G. True; in the pauper's grand inebriate wish
 To know what wealth is,—tho' but for an hour.
Lady M. But blame you me or mine, if spendthrift wassail
 Run to the dregs? Mine halls stand open to you;
 My noble Beaufort hath not spurned your converse;
 You have been welcomed——.
Sir G.   At your second table,
 And as the butt of unchastised lackeys;,
 While your kind son, in pity of my want,
 Hath this day killed the faithful dog that shared it.
 'Tis well; you need my aid, as did your father,
 And tempt, like him, with gold. I take the service;
 And, when the task is done will talk of payment.
 Hist! the boughs rustle. Closer space were safer;
 Vouchsafe your hand, let us confer within.
Lady M. Well might I dream last night! A fearful dream.
 [*Exeunt* Lady Montreville *and* Sir Grey, *by steps, and off* R. 2. E.
  conversing.
      Enter Eveline, L. 2 E.

Evel. Oh, for some fairy talisman to conjure
 Up to these longing eyes the form they pine for!
 And yet, in love, there's no such word as absence;
 The loved one glides beside our steps forever; (*seated in garden*
  seat.)
 Its presence gave such beauty to the world,
 That all things beautiful its tokens are,
 And aught in sound most sweet, to sight most fair,
 Breathes with its voice, and haunts us with its aspect.

      Enter Vyvyan, L. 3 E.

 There spoke my fancy, not my heart! Where art thou,
 My unforgotten Vyvyan?
Vyv. (*kneels to her*).   At thy feet!
 Look up—look up!—these are the arms that sheltered
 When the storm howled around; and these the lips
 Where, till this hour, the sad and holy kiss
 Of parting lingered, as the fragance left
 By angels, when they touch the earth and vanish.
 Look up; night never hungered for the sun
 As for thine eyes my soul!

EVEL. (*embraces* VYVYAN).   Oh! joy, joy, joy!

VYV. Yet weeping still, tho' leaning on my breast!
My sailor's bride, hast thou no voice but blushes?
Nay from those drooping roses let me steal
The coy reluctant sweetness!

EVEL.   And, methought
I had treasured words, 'twould take a life to utter
When we should meet again!

VYV.   Recall them later.
We shall have time eno', when life with life
Blends into one;—(EVELINE *looks* R.) why dost thou start and
          tremble?

EVEL. Methought I heard her slow and solemn footfall! (*rises.*)

VYV. *Her!* Why, thou speak'st of woman: the meek word
Which never chimes with terror.

EVEL.   You know not
The dame of Montreville. (c.)

VYV. (R. *of* EVELINE).   Is she so stern?

EVEL. Not stern, but haughty; as if high-born virtue
Swept o'er the earth to scorn the faults it pardoned.

VYV. Haughty to thee?

EVEL.   To all, e'en when the kindest;
Nay, I do wrong her; never to her son;
And when those proud eyes moisten as they hail him,
Hearts lately stung, yearn to a heart so human!
Alas, that parent love! how in its loss
All life seems shelterless!

VYV.   Like thee, perchance,
Looking round earth for that same parent shelter,
I too may find but tombs. So, turn we both,
Orphans, to that lone parent of the lonely,
That doth like Sorrow ever upward gaze
On calm consoling stars; the mother Sea.

EVEL. Call not the cruel sea by that mild name.

VYV. She is not cruel if her breast swell high
Against the winds that thwart her loving aim
To link, by every raft whose course she speeds,
Man's common brotherhood from pole to pole;
Grant she hath danger—danger schools the brave,
And bravery leaves all cruel things to cowards.
Grant that she harden us to fear, the hearts
Most proof to fear are easiest moved to love,
As on the oak whose roots defy the storm,
All the leaves tremble when the south-wind stirs.
Yet if the sea dismay thee, (*right arm around* EVELINE's *waist*)
          on the shores
Kissed by her waves, and far, as fairy isles
In poet dreams, from this gray care-worn world,
Blooms many a bower for the Sea Rover's bride.
I know a land where feathering palm-trees shade
To delicate twilight, suns benign as those
Whose dawning gilded Eden; Nature, there,
Like a gay spendthrift in his flush of youth,
Flings her whole treasure on the lap of Time.
There, steeped in roseate hues, the lakelike sea
Heaves to an air whose breathing is ambrosia;
And, all the while, bright-winged and warbling birds,

Like happy souls released, melodious ffoat
Thro' blissful light, and teach the ravished earth
How joy finds voice in Heaven.   Come, rest we yonder,
And, side by side, forget that we are orphans!
                    [VYVYAN *and* EVELINE *exeunt,* L. 1 E.

Enter LADY MONTREVILLE *and* SIR GREY, R. 2 E., *and down the steps.*

LADY M. Yet still, if Alton sees——
SIR G.   Without the proofs,
    Why, Alton's story were but idle wind ;
    The man I send is swift and strong, and ere
    This Vyvyan (who would have been here before me
    But that I took the shorter path) depart
    From your own threshold to the priest's abode,
    Our agent gains the solitary dwelling,
    And——
LADY M. But no violence !
SIR G.   Nay, none but fear—
    Fear will suffice to force from trembling age
    Your safety, and preserve your Beaufort's birthright.
LADY M. Let me not hear the ignominious means ;
    Gain thou the end ;—quick—quick !
SIR G.   And if, meanwhile,
    This sailor come, be nerved to meet a stranger ;
    And to detain a guest.
LADY M.   My heart is wax,
    But my will, iron.—Go. (R. C. *by seat.*)
SIR G. (*aside.*)   To fear add force—
    And this hand closes on the proofs, and welds
    That iron to a tool.   [*Exit* SIR GREY, R. I E.

Enter VYVYAN *and* EVELINE, L. 1 E., *to up* L. C.

EVEL.   Nay, Vyvyan—nay,
    Your guess can fathom not how proud her temper.
VYV. Tut for her pride ! a king upon the deck
    Is every subject's equal in the hall.
    I will advance. (*he uncovers.*)
LADY M.   Avenging angels, spare me !
                    (*great emotion, unable to look at* VYVYAN.]
VYV. Pardon the seeming boldness of my presence.
EVEL.* Our gallant countryman, of whom my father
    So often spake—who from the Algerine
    Rescued our lives and freedom.
LADY M.   Ah ! Your name, sir?
VYV. The name I bear is Vyvyan, noble lady.
LADY M. Sir, you are welcome. Walk within, and hold
    Our home your hostel, while it lists you.
VYV.   Madam,
    I shall be prouder in all after time
    For having been your guest.
LADY M   How love and dread

| *LADY M.* | VYVYAN. | EVELINE. |
| R. *of* C. | C. | L. C. |

Make tempest here!   I pray you follow me.
                    [*Exit* LADY MONTREVILLE, R. 2 E.

Vyv.   A most majestic lady—her fair face
       Made my heart tremble, and called back old dreams:
       Thou saidst she had a son?
Evel.   Ah, yes.
Vyv.   In truth
       A happy man.
Evel.   Yet he might envy thee:
Vyv.   Most arch reprover, yes.   As kings themselves
       Might envy one whose arm entwines his all.
                    [*arm around* EVELINE, *exeunt* R. 2 E.   *Music.*

CURTAIN.

———

ACT II.

SCENE I.—*Room in 1st grooves.*

Discover LADY MONTREVILLE *and* VYVYAN *seated at table, and* EVELINE
L. C. *front.**

Vyv.   Ha! ha!   In truth we made a scurvy figure
       After our shipwreck.
Lady M.   You jest merrily
       On your misfortunes.
Vyv.   'Tis the way with sailors:
       Still in extremes.   Ah! I can be sad sometimes.
Lady M. That sigh, in truth, speaks sadness.   Sir, if I
       In aught could serve you, trust me.
Evel.   Trust her, Vyvyan.
       Methinks the mournful tale of thy young years
       Would raise thee up a friend, wherever pity
       Lives in the heart of woman.
Vyv.   Gentle lady,
       The key of some charmed music in your voice
       Unlocks a haunted chamber in my soul;
       And—would you listen to an outcast's tale,
       'Tis briefly told.   Until my fifteenth year,
       Beneath the roof of a poor village priest,
       Not far from hence, my childhood wore away;
       Then stirred within me restless thoughts and deep;
       Throughout the liberal and harmonious nature
       Something seemed absent,—what, I scarcely knew,
       Till one calm night, when over slumbering seas
       Watched the still heaven, and down on every wave
       Looked some soft lulling star—the instinctive want
       Learned what it pined for; and I asked the priest
       With a quick sigh—" Why I was motherless?"

————————

LADY M.*: table.   :*VYVYAN.
                              *EVELINE.

LADY M. And he ?—

VYV.   Replied that—I was nobly born,
And that the cloud which dimmed a dawning sun,
Oft but feretold its splendor at the noon.
As thus he spoke, faint memories struggling came—
Faint as the things some former life hath known.

LADY M. Of what?

VYV. (*rises, keeps his eyes on* LADY M.). A face sweet with a stately
        sorrow,
And lips which breathed the words that mothers murmur.

LADY M. (*aside*). Back, tell-tale tears ! (*weeping*.)

VYV.   About that time, a stranger
Came to our hamlet ; rough, yet, some said, well-born ;
Roysterer, and comrade, such as youth delights in.
Sailor he called himself, and naught belied
The sailor's metal ringing in his talk
Of El Dorados, and Enchanted Isles,
Of hardy Raleigh, and of dauntless Drake,
And great Columbus with prophetic eyes
Fixed on a dawning world.   His legends fired me—
And, from the deep whose billows washed our walls,
The alluring wave called with a Siren's music.
And thus I left my home with that wild seaman.

LADY M. The priest, consenting; still divulged not more ?

VYV. No; nor rebuked mine ardor. " Go," he said,
" The noblest of all nobles are the men
In whom their country feels herself ennobled."

LADY M. (*aside*). I breathe again. (*aloud*) Well, thus you left these
        shores——

VYV. Scarce had the brisker sea-wind filled our sails,
When the false traitor who had lured my trust '
Cast me to chains and darkness.   Days went by,
At length—one belt of desolate waters round,
And on the decks one scowl of swarthy brows,
(A hideous crew, the refuse of all shores)—
Under the flapping of his raven flag
The pirate stood revealed, and called his captive.
Grimly he heard my boyish loud upbraidings,
And grimly smiled in answering: " I, like thee,
Cast off, and disinherited, and desperate,
Had but one choice, death or the pirate's flag—
Choose *thou*—I am more gracious than thy kindred ;
I proffer life; the gold *they* gave me paid
Thy grave in ocean ! "

LADY M.   Hold ! The demon lied !

VYV. Swift, as I answered so, his blade flashed forth ;
But self-defence is swifter still than slaughter ;
I plucked a sword from one who stood beside me,
        (*gesture of parrying a thrust and replying by a down cut*)
And smote the slanderer to my feet.   Then all
That human hell broke loose ; oaths rang, steel lightened ;
When in the death-swoon of the caitiff chief,
The pirate next in rank forced back the swarm,
And—in that superstition of the sea
Which makes the sole religion of its outlaws—
Forbade my doom by bloodshed—griped and bound me
To a slight plank ; spread to the winds the sail,

And left me on the waves alone with God.

EVEL. Pause. (*standing beside* VYVYAN) Let my hand take thine—
  its warm life,
  And, shuddering less, thank Him whose eye was o'er thee.

VYV. That day, and all that night, upon the seas
  Tossed the frail barrier between life and death;
  Heaven lulled the gales; and when the stars came forth,
  All looked so bland and gentle that I wept,
  Recalled that wretch's words, and murmured, "All,
  E'en wave and wind, are kinder than my kindred!"
  But—nay, sweet lady——

LADY M. (*sobbing*).   Heed me not. (*with an effort*) Night passed

VYV. Day dawned; and, glittering in the sun, behold
  A sail—a flag!

EVEL.   Well—well?

VYV.   Like Hope, it vanished!
  Noon glaring came—with noon came thirst and famine,
  And with parched lips I called on death, and sought
  To wrench my limbs from the stiff cords that gnawed
  Into the flesh, and drop into the deep:
  And then—the clear wave trembled, and below
  I saw a dark, swift-moving, shapeless thing,
  With watchful, glassy eyes;—the ghastly shark
  Swam hungering round its prey—then life once more
  Grew sweet, and with a strained and horrent gaze
  And lifted hair I floated on, till sense
  Grew dim, and dimmer; and a terrible sleep
  (In which still—still those livid eyes met mine)
  Fell on me—and——

EVEL.   Quick—quick!

VYV.   I woke, and heard
  My native tongue! Kind looks were bent upon me.
  I lay on deck—escaped the ravening death—
  For God had watched the sleeper.

EVEL.   Oh, such memories
  Make earth, forever after, nearer heaven;
  And each new hour an altar for thanksgiving.

LADY M. Break not the tale my ear yet strains to listen.

VYV. True lion of the ocean was the chief
  Of that good ship. Beneath his fostering eyes,
  Nor all ungraced by Drake's illustrious praise,
  And the frank clasp of Raleigh's kingly hand,
  I fought my way to manhood. At his death
  The veteran left me a more absolute throne
  Than Cæsar filled—his war-ship; for my realm
  Add to the ocean, hope—and measure it!
  Nameless, I took his name. My tale is done—
  And each past sorrow, like a wave on shore,
  Dies on this golden hour. (*goes* L. *with* EVELINE, *tenderly.*)

LADY M. (*observing them*).   He loves my ward,
  Whom Clarence, too—that thought piles fear on fear;
  Yet, hold—that very rivalship gives safety—
  Affords pretext to urge the secret nuptials,
  And the prompt parting, ere he meet with Alton.
  I—but till Nature sobs itself to peace,
  Here's that which chokes all reason. Will ye not

Taste summer air, cooled through yon shadowy alleys?
Anon I'll join you.   [*Exit* LADY MONTREVILLE, R.
VYV.   We will wait your leisure.
A most compassionate and courteous lady—
How could'st thou call her proud?
EVEL.   Nay, ever henceforth,
For the soft pity she has shown to thee,
I'll love her as a mother.
VYV.   Thus I thank thee. (*kissing her hand.*)
                                    [*Exeunt* L.

SCENE II.—*Castle yard, in 5th grooves.*

Enter SIR GREY DE MALPAS, L. 1 E.

LORD B. (*speaking off* L. 2 E.). A noble falcon! Marsden, hood him
    gently.

Enter LORD BEAUFORT, D. *in* 3 G. *set.*

Good-day, old knight, thou hast a lowering look,
As if still ruffled by some dire affray
With lawless mice, at riot in thy larder.
SIR G. Mice in my house! magnificent dreamer, mice!
The last was found three years ago last Christmas,
Stretched out beside a bone; so lean and worn
With pious fast—'twas piteous to behold it;
I canonized its corpse in spirits of wine,
And set it in the porch—a solemn warning
To its poor cousins! (*aside*) Shall I be avenged?
He killed my dog too.

Enter VYVYAN *and* EVELINE, R. 2 E., *remaining up* R. *on platform.*

LORD B. (L. C.).   Knight, look here!—A stranger,
And whispering with my cousin.
SIR G. (L. C. *front, aside*).   Jealous? Ha!
Something should come of this: Hail, green-eyed fiend!
(*aloud*) Let us withdraw—tho' old, I have been young;
The whispered talk of lovers should be sacred.
LORD B. Lovers!
SIR G.   Ah! true! You know not, in you absence
Your mother hath received a welcome guest
In your fair cousin's wooer. Note him well,
A stalwart, comely gallant.
LORD B.   Art thou serious?
A wooer to my cousin—quick, his name!
SIR G. His name?—my memory doth begin to fail me—
Your mother will recall it. Seek—ask *her*——
                    (VYVYAN *and* EVELINE *come down* R. C.)
LORD B. (*to* C.). Whom have we here? Familiar sir, excuse me,
I do not see the golden spurs of knighthood.
VYV.* Alack, we sailors have not so much gold
That we should waste it on our heels! The steeds
We ride to battle need no spurs, Sir Landsman;

---

	* EVELINE.	VYVYAN.	BEAUFORT.	SIR GREY.
	R. *of* C.	C.		L. C.

LORD B. And overleap all laws; (*sneeringly*) methinks thou art
    One of those wild Sea Rovers, who——
VYV. (*quickly*).   Refuse
    To yield to Spain's pround tyranny, her claim
    To treat as thieves and pirates all who cross
    The line Spain's finger draws across God's ocean.
    We, the Sea Rovers, on our dauntless decks
    Carry our land, its language, laws, and freedom;
    We wrest from Spain the sceptre of the seas,
    And in the New World build up a new England.
    For this high task, if we fulfill it duly,
    The Old and New World both shall bless the names
    Of Walter Raleigh and his bold Sea Rovers.
LORD B. Of those names thine is——
VYV.   Vyvyan.
LORD B.   .   Master Vyvyan,
    Our rank scarce fits us for a fair encounter
    With the loud talk of blustering mariners.
    We bar you not our hospitality;
    Our converse, yes. Go ask the Seneschal
    To lodge you with your equals !
VYV.   Equals, stripling !
    Mine equals truly should be bearded men,
    Noble with titles carpet lords should bow to——
    Memories of dangers dared, and service done,
    And scars on bosoms that have bled for England !
SIR G. Nay, coz, he has thee there. (*restraining* BEAUFORT *from draw-
    ing sword.*)
                      Thou shalt not, Clarence.
    Strike *me.* I'm weak and safe——but *he* is dangerous.

Enter LADY MONTREVILLE, R. 1 E., *as* LORD BEAUFORT *breaks from* SIR
    GREY *and draws his sword.*

EVEL. Protect your guest from your rash son.
LADY M.   Thy sword
    Drawn on thy——(c.) Back, boy ! I command thee, back!
    To you, sir guest, have I in aught so failed,
    That in the son you would rebuke the mother ?
VYV.* Madam, believe, my sole offence was this,
    That rated as a serf, I spoke as man.
LADY M. Wherefore, Lord Beaufort, such unseemly humors ?
LORD B. (*drawing her aside*). Wherefore ?—and while we speak his
          touch profanes her !
    Who is this man ? Dost thou approve his suit ?
    Beware !
LADY M.   You would not threaten——Oh, my Clarence,
    Hear me—you——
LORD B.   Learned in childhood from my mother
    To brook no rival—and to curb no passion.
    Aid'st thou you scatterling against thy son,
    Where most his heart is set ?
LADY M.   Thy heart, perverse one ?
    Thou saidst it was not love.

---

*EVELINE.	VYVYAN.	LADY M.	BEAUFORT.	SIR GREY.
R.	R. C.	C.	L. C.	L.

LORD B.   That was before
   A rival made it love—nay, fear not mother,
   If you dismiss this insolent; but, mark me,
   Dismiss him straight, or by mine honor, madam,
   Blood will be shed.

LADY B.   Thrice miserable boy!
   Let the heavens hear thee not!

LORD B. (*whispering to* VYVYAN *as he crosses* R.) Again, and soon, sir!
                                  [*Exit* R. 1 E.

LADY M. (*seeing* SIR GREY). Villain!—but no, I dare not yet up-
   braid——
   (*aloud*) After him, quick! Appease, soothe, humor him.

SIR G. Ay, madam, trust to your poor cousin.   [*Exit* R. 1 E.

LADY M.   Eveline, ,
   Thou lov'st this Vyvyan?

EVEL.   Lady—I—he saved
   My life and honor.

LADY M.   Leave us, gentle child,
   I would confer with him. May both be happy!

EVEL. (*to* VYVYAN). Hush! she consents; well mayst then bid me
   love her.   [*Exit* EVELINE, L. 1 E.

LADY M. Sir, if I gather rightly from your speech,
   You do not mean long sojourn on these shores?

VYV. Lady, in sooth, mine errand here was two-fold.
   First, to behold, and, if I dare assume
   That you will ratify her father's promise,
   To claim my long affianced; next to learn
   If Heaven vouchsafe me yet a parent's heart.
   I gained these shores to hear of war and danger—
   The long-suspended thunderbolt of Spain
   Threatened the air. I have dispatched an envoy
   To mine old leader, Drake, to crave sure tidings;
   I wait reply: If England be in peril,
   Hers my first service; if, as rumor runs,
   The cloud already melts without a storm,
   Then, my bride gained, and my birth tracked, I sail
   Back to the Indian seas, where wild adventure
   Fulfills in life what boyhood dreamed in song.

LADY M. 'Tis frankly spoken—frankly I reply.
   First—England's danger; now, for five slow years
   Have Spain's dull trumpets blared their braggart war,
   And Rome's gray monk-craft muttered new crusades;
   Well, we live still—and all this deluge dies
   In harmless spray on England's scornful cliffs.
   And, trust me, sir, if war beleaguer England,
   Small need of one man's valor: lacked she soldiers,
   Methinks a Mars would strike in childhood's arm,
   And woman be Bellona!

VYV.   Stately matron,
   So would our mother country speak and look,
   Could she take visible image!

LADY M.   Claim thy bride
   With my assent, and joyous gratulation.
   She shall not go undowried to your arms.
   Nor deem me wanting to herself and you
   If I adjure prompt nuptials and departure.
   Beaufort—thou see'st how fiery is his mood—

In my ward's lover would avenge a rival :
Indulge the impatient terrors of a mother,
And quit these shores. Why not this night ?

Vyv.   This night ?
With her—my bride ?

Lady M.   So from the nuptial altar
Pledge thou thy faith to part—to spread the sail
And put wide seas between my son and thee.

Vyv. This night, with Eveline !—dream of rapture ! (*changes look from
      joy to pain*) yet—
My birth untracked—

Lady M.   Delay not for a doubt
Bliss when assured. And, heed me, I have wealth
To sharpen law. and power to strengthen justice ;
I will explore the mazes of this mystery ;
I—I will track your parents.

Vyv.   Blessed lady ;
My parents !—Find me one with eyes like thine,
                          (Lady M. *starts*.)
And were she lowliest of the hamlet born,
I would not change with monarchs.

Lady M. (*aside*).   Can I bear this ?
Your Eveline well nigh is my daughter ; you
Her plighted spouse ; pray you this kiss—O sweet !
      (Vyvyan *sinks on one knee as* Lady M. *kisses his forehead*.)

Vyv. Ah, as I kneel, and as thou bendest o'er me,
Methinks an angel's hand lifts up the veil
Of Time, the great magician and I see
Above mine infant couch, a face like thine.

Lady M. Mine, stranger !

Vyv.   Pardon me ; a vain wild thought
I know it is ; but on my faith, I think
My mother was like thee.

Lady M.   Peace, peace ! We talk
And fool grave hours away. Inform thy bride ;
Then to thy bark, and bid thy crew prepare ;
Meanwhile, I give due orders to my chaplain.
Beside the altar we shall meet once more ;—
(*voice breaks*) And then—and then—Heaven's blessing and farewell !
                          [*Exit* Lady Montreville, L. 1 E., *wildly*.

Vyv. Most feeling heart ! its softness hath contagion,
And melts mine own ! Her aspect wears a charm
That half divides my soul with Eveline's love !
Strange ! while I muse, a chill and ominous awe
Creeps thro' my veins ! Away, ye vague forebodings !
Eveline ! At thy dear name the phantoms vanish,
And the glad future breaks like land on sea,
When rain-mists melt beneath the golden morn.

                          Enter, D. *in* 3 G. *set,* Falkner.

Falk. Ha! Vyvyan !
Vyv.   Thou !
Falk.   Breathless with speed to reach thee.
I guessed thee lingering here. Thy foster sire
Hath proofs that clear the shadow from thy birth.
Go—he awaits thee where you cloud-capt rock

Jags air with barbed peaks—St. Kinian's Cliff.

[*Shouts off* L., *faintly.*

Vyv. My birth! My parents live?

FALK.   I know no more.

Enter, D. *in* 3 G. *set*, HARDING.

HARD. Captain, the rumor lied. I bring such news
As drums and clarions and resounding anvils
Fashioning the scythes of reapers into swords,
Shall ring from Thames to Tweed.

Vyv.   The foeman comes!

HARD. (*gives letter*). These lines will tell thee ; Drake's own hand.

[*Goes up* L. C,

Vyv. (*reads*).   "The Armada
Has left the Groyne, and we are ranging battle.
Come ! in the van I leave one gap for thee."
Poor Eveline ! Shame on such unworthy weakness !

FALK. Time to see her and keep thy tryst with Alton.
Leave me to call the crews and arm the decks.
Not till the moon rise, in the second hour
After the sunset, will the deepening tide
Float us from harbor—ere that hour be past
Our ship shall wait thee by St. Kinian's Cliff.
Small need to pray thee not to miss the moment
Whose loss would lose thee honor.

Vyv.   If I come not
Ere the waves reel to thy third signal gun,
Deem Death alone could so delay from duty,
And step into my post as o'er my corpse.

FALK. Justly, my captain. thou rebuk'st my warning,
And couldst thou fail us, I would hold the signal
As if thy funeral knell—crowd every sail,
And know thy soul——

Vyv.   Was with my country still. (*shouts off* L.)

Enter, D. *in* 3 G. *set*, SUB-OFFICER, SAILORS, RETAINERS, *and* VILLAGERS,
confusedly.

SUB-OFFICER (*with broadsheet*). Captain, look here. Just come!

Vyv.   The Queen's Address
From her own lips to the armed lines at Tilbury.

VOICES. Read it, sir, read it—

Vyv.   Hush then. (*reads*) " Loving people,
Let tyrants fear ! I, under Heaven, have placed
In loyal hearts my chiefest strength and safeguard,
Being resolved in the midst and heat of the battle
To live and die amongst you all ; content
To lay down for my God and for my people
My life blood even in the dust : I know
I have the body of a feeble woman,
But a King's heart a King of England's too ;
And think foul scorn that Parma, Spain, or Europe,
Dare to invade the borders of my realm !
Where England fights—with concord in the camp,
Trust in the chief, and valor in the field,

Swift be her victory over every foe
Threatening her crown, her altars, and her people."

The noble Woman King ! These words of fire
Will send warm blood through all the veins of Freedom
Till England is a dream ! Uncover, lads !
God and St. George ! Hurrah for England's Queen !
(Cheers, all cheer.)

VILLAGERS. *   *   *   *   *   * VILLAGERS.
FALKNER.*   *VYVYAN. *HARDING.

· QUICK CURTAIN.

ACT III.

SCENE I.—*Rocky Landscape in 2d grooves.*

Discover ALTON *and* VYVYAN, *seated* C.

ALTON. And I believed them when they said "He died
  In the far seas."   Ten years of desolate sorrow
  Passed as one night—Now thy warm hand awakes me.
VYV. Dear friend, the sun sets fast.
ALTON.   Alas ! then listen.
  There was a page, fair, gentle, brave, but low-born—
  And in those years when, to young eyes the world,
  With all the rough disparities of fortune,
  Floats level thro' the morning haze of fancy,
  He loved the heiress of a lordly house :
  She scarce from childhood, listening, loved again,
  And secret nuptials hallowed stolen meetings—
  'Till one—I know not whom (perchance a kinsman,
  Heir to that house—if childless died its daughter)
  Spied—tracked the bridegroom to the bridal bower,
  Aroused the sire, and said, "Thy child's dishonored !"
  Snatching his sword, the father sought the chamber ;
  Burst the closed portal—but his lifted hand
  Escaped the crime.   Cold as a fallen statue,
  Cast from its blessed pedestal forever,
  The bride lay senseless on the lonely floor
  By the ope'd casement, from whose terrible height
  The generous boy, to save her life or honor,
  Had plunged into his own sure death below.
VYV. A happy death, if it saved her he loved !
ALTON. A midnight grave concealed the mangled clay,
  And buried the bride's secret. Few nights after,
  Darkly as life from him had passed away,
  Life dawned on thee—and, from the unconscious mother,
  Stern hands conveyed the pledge of fatal nuptials
  To the poor priest, who to thy loftier kindred
  Owed the mean roof that sheltered thee.

Vyv.   Oh, say
    I have a mother still !
Alton.   Yes !
Vyv. (*with joy*).   Oh !
Alton.   She survived—
    Her vows, thy birth, by the blind world unguessed;
    And, after years of woe and vain resistance,
    Forced to a lordlier husband's arms.
Vyv.   "My soul
    Ofttimes recalls a shadowy mournfulness,
    With woman's patient brow, and saddest tears
    Dropped fast from woman's eyes ;—they were my mother's.
Alton. In stealth a wife—in stealth a mother! yes,
    Then did she love thee, *then* aspired to own
    In coming times, and bade me hoard these proofs
    For that blest day." Alas ! new ties
    Brought new affections—to the second nuptials
    A second son was born; she loved him better,
    Better than thee—than her own soul !
Vyv.   Poor mother !
Alton. And haughtier thoughts on riper life arose,
    And worldly greatness feared the world's dread shame.
    And she forsook her visits to thy pillow,
    And the sire threatened, and the kinsman prayed,
    Till, over-urged by terror for thy safety,
    I took reluctant vows to mask the truth
    And hush thy rights while lived thy mother's sire
    And he, her second unsuspecting lord.
    Thus thy youth, nameless, left my lonely roof.
    The sire and husband died while thou wert absent.
    Thou liv'st—thou hast returned ; mine oath is freed;
    These scrolls attest my tale and prove thy birthright—
    Hail, Lord of Beaufort—Heir of Montreville !
Vyv. 'Tis she—'tis she ! At the first glance I loved her !
    And when I told my woes, she wept—she wept !
    This is her writing. Look—look where she calls me
    " Edmond and child." Old man, how thou hast wronged her !
    Joy—joy ! I fly to claim and find a mother !
                      [*Exit* Vyvyan, L. 1 e.
Alton. Just power, propitiate Nature to that cry.
    "And from the hardened rock, let living streams
    Gush as in Horeb ! Ah, how faintly flags,
    Strained by unwonted action, weary age !
    I'll seek the neighboring hamlet—rest and pray."
                      [*Exit* Alton, R. 1 e.

SCENE II.—*Castle Exterior as in* Scene II., *Act II.* Sunset.

Enter Sir Grey *and* Wrecklyffe, d. *in* 3 g. flat.

Sir G. The priest has left his home ?
Wreck.   The hour I reached it.
Sir G. With but one man ? Did'st thou not hound the foot-track ?
Wreck. I did.
Sir G.   Thou didst—and yet the prey escaped !
    I have done. I gave thee thy soul's wish, revenge,
    Revenge on Vyvyan—and thou leav'st his way

Clear to a height as high from thy revenge
As is yon watch-tower from a pirate's gibbet.
WRECK. Silence! thou——
SIR. G. (*haughtily*).   Sir!
WRECK. (*subdued and cowed*). Along the moors I track'd them.
 But only came in sight and reach of spring
 Just as they gained the broad and thronging road,
 . Aloud with eager strides, and clamorous voices—
 A surge of tumult, wave to wave re booming
 . How all the might of Parma and of Spain
 Hurried its thunders on. (*gas gradually down during this scene.*)
SIR G.   Dolt, what to us
 Parma and Spain ?   The beggar has no country !
WRECK. But deeds like that which thou dost urge me to
 Are not risked madly in the populous day.
 I come to thy sharp wit for safer orders.
SIR G. My wit is dulled by time, and must be ground
 Into an edge by thought.   Hist !—the door jars,
 She comes.   Skulk yonder—hide thee—but in call !
 A moment sometimes makes or marreth fortune,
 Just as the fiend Occasion springs to hand—
 Be *thou* that fiend !   [WRECKLYFFE *exits up* R. C.

Enter LADY MONTREVILLE, L. 1 E.

LADY M.   Look on me ! What, nor tremble ?
 Couldst thou have deemed my father's gold a bribe
 For my son's murder ?   Sold to pirates ! Cast
 On the wild seas !
SIR G.   How ! I knew naught of this.
 If such the truth, peace to thy father's sins,
 For of those sins is this.   Let the past sleep,
 Meet present ills—the priest hath left his home
 With Vyvyan's comrade, and our scheme is foiled.
LADY M. I will, myself, see Alton on the morrow—
 Edmond can scarce forestall me ; for this night
 Fear sails with him to the far Indian main.
SIR G. Let me do homage to thy genius.   Sorceress,
 What was thy magic ?
LADY M.   Terror for my Clarence,
 And Edmond's love for Eveline.
SIR G. (*aside*).   I see !
 Bribed by the prize of which she robs his rival !
 This night—so soon ?—this night—
LADY M.   I save my Clarence !
 Till then, keep close, close to his side. Thou hast soothed him ?
SIR G. Fear not—these sudden tidings of the foe
 With larger fires have paled receding love—
 But where is Vyvyan ?
LADY M.   Doubtless with his crew,
 Preparing for departure.
LORD B. (*without*   This way, Marsden.

Enter, L. 2 E., LORD BEAUFORT, *with* MARSDEN *and armed* ATTENDANTS:

LORD B. (*to* R.) Repair yon broken parapets at dawn ;
 Yonder the culverins ,—delve down more sharply

That bank ;—clear out the moat. Those trees—eh—Marsden,
Should fall ? They'd serve to screen the foe ! (*comes to* c.) Ah,
mother,
Make me a scarf to wear above the armor
In which thy father, 'mid the shouts of kings,
Shivered French lances at the Cloth of Gold.

MARS. Nay, my young lord, too vast for you that armor.

LORD B. No ; you forget that the breast swells in danger,
And honor adds a cubit to the stature.

LADY M. Embrace me, Clarence, I myself will arm thee.
Look at him, Marsden—yet they say I spoil him !

SIR G. (*draws* LADY M. *to* L. c., *and whispers*). I mark i' the distance,
swift disordered strides,
And the light bound of an impatient spirit ;
Vyvyan speeds hither, and the speed seems joy.
He sought his crew—Alton might there await him.

LADY M. His speed is to a bride.

SIR G.   Ay, true—old age
Forgets that Love's as eager as Ambition ;
Yet hold thyself prepared.

LADY M. (*to herself.*)   And if it were so !
Come, I will sound the depths of Beaufort's heart !
And, as that answers, hush or yield to conscience.
Lead off these men.
    [*Exeunt* SIR GREY *and* ATTENDANTS, D. *in* 3 G. *flat.*
(*to* MARSDEN)   Go, meet my this day's guest,
And see he enter through the garden postern.
    [*Exit* MARSDEN, L. 1 E.

Clarence, come back.

LORD B. (*peevishly.*) What now ? (R.)

LADY M.   Speak kindly, Clarence.
Alas, thou'lt know not till the grave close o'er me,
How I did need thy kindness !

LORD B.   Pardon, mother,
My blunt speech now, and froward heat this morning.

LADY M. Be all such follies of the past, as leaves
Shed from the petals of the bursting flower.
Think thy soul slept, till honor's sudden dawn
Flashed, and the soil bloomed with one hero more !
Ah, Clarence, had I, too, an elder-born,
As had thy father by his former nuptials !—
Could thy sword carve out fortune ?

LORD B.   Ay, my mother !

LADY M. "Well the bold answer rushes from thy lips !"
Yet, tell me frankly, dost thou not, in truth,
Prize over much the outward show of things ;
And couldst thou—rich with valor, health and beauty,
And hope—the priceless treasure of the young—
Couldst thou endure descent from that vain height
Where pride builds towers the heart inhabits not ;
To live less gorgeously, and curb thy wants
Within the state, not of the heir to earls,
But of a simple gentleman ?

LORD B.   If reared to it,
Perchance contented so ; but *now*—no, never !
Such as I am, thy lofty self hath made me ;
Ambitious, haughty, prodigal ; and pomp

A part of my very life. If I could fall
From my high state, it were as Romans fell,
On their swords' point!
LADY M. (*in horror*).   Oh!
LORD B.   Why is your cheek so hueless?
Why daunt yourself with airiest fantasies?
Who can deprive me of mine heritage—
"The titles borne at Palestine and Crecy?
The seignory, ancient as the throne it guards,"
That will be mine in trust for sons unborn,
When time—from this day may the date be far!—
Transfers the circlet on thy stately brows
(Forgive the boast!) to no unworthy heir.
LADY M. (*aside*). My proud soul speaks in his, and stills remorse;
I'll know no other son! Now go, Lord Beaufort.
LORD B. So formal—fie!—has Clarence then offended?
LADY M. Offended?—thou! Resume thy noble duties,
Sole heir of Montreville!   [*Exit* LORD BEAUFORT, L. 2 E.
My choice is made.
As one who holds a fortress for his king,
I guard this heart for Clarence, and I close
Its gates against the stranger. Let him come.
[*Exit*, L. 1. E.

Enter, D. *in* 3 G. *flat*, VYVYAN *and* EVELINE.

EVEL. I would not bid thee stay, thy country calls thee—
But thou hast stunned my heart i' the midst of joy
With this dread sudden word—part—part!
VYV.   Live not
In the brief present. Go forth to the future!
Wouldst thou not see me worthier of thy love?
EVEL. Thou canst not be so.
VYV.   Sweet one, I am now
Obscure and nameless. What if at thy feet
I could lay rank and fortune?
EVEL.   These could give
To me no bliss save as they bless thyself.
Into the life of him she loves, the life
Of woman flows, and nevermore reflects
Sunshine or shadow on a separate wave.
Be his lot great, for his sake she loves greatness;
Humble—a cot with *him* is Arcady!
Thou art ambitious; thou wouldst arm for fame,
Fame then fires me too, and without a tear
I bid thee go where fame is won—as now:
Win it and I rejoice; but fail to win,
Were it not joy to think I could console?
VYV. Oh, that I could give vent to this full heart!
Time rushes on, each glimmering star rebukes me—
Is that the Countess yonder? This way—come. (*up* C.)
[*Moonlight falls on* L. *side now.*

Enter LORD BEAUFORT *and* SIR GREY, L. 1 E.

LORD B. Leave England, say'st thou—and with her?
SIR G.   Thou hast wrung

The secret from me.   Mark—I have thy promise
Not to betray me to thy mother.

LORD B.   Ah !
Thought she to dupe me with that pomp of words,
And blind ambition while she beggar'd life ?
No, by yon heavens, she shall not so befool me !

SIR G. Be patient.   Had I guessed how this had galled,
I had been dumb.

LORD B.   Stand from the light !   Distraction !
She hangs upon his breast ! ·(*hurries to* VYVYAN, *and then un-
covering with an attempt at courtesy, draws him to front.*)

LORD B.   Sir, one word with you.
This day such looks and converse passed between us
As men who wear these vouchers for esteem,
Cancel with deeds.

VYV. (*aside*).   The brave boy !   How I love him !

LORD B. What saidst thou, sir ?

EVEL. (*approaching*).   Oh, Clarence.

LORD B.   Fear not, cousin.
I do but make excuses for my rudeness
At noon, to this fair cavalier.

SIR G.   If so,
Let us not mar such courteous purpose, lady.

EVEL. But—

SIR G.   Nay, you are too timid ! (*draws* EVELINE *up* L.)

LORD B.   Be we brief, sir.
You quit these parts to-night.   This place beseems not
The only conference we should hold.   I pray you
Name spot and hour in which to meet again,
Unwitnessed save by the broad early moon.

VYV. Meet thee again—oh, yes !

LORD B.   There speaks a soldier,
And now I own an equal.   Hour and place ?

VYV. Wait here till I have——

LORD B.   No, sir, on thy road.
Here we are spied.

VYV.   So be it, on my road.
(*aside*) [There where I learned that heaven had given a brother,
There the embrace.]   Within the hour I pass
St. Kinan's Cliff.

LORD B.   Alone ?

VYV.   Alone.

LORD B. Farewell !

SIR. G. (*catching at* LORD BEAUFORT *as he goes out.*) I heard St
Kinian's Cliff.   I'll warn the Countess.

LORD B. Do it, and famish !

SIR G.   Well, thy fence is skillful.

LORD B. And my hand firm.

SIR G.   But when ?

LORD B.   Within the hour !
[*Exit* LORD BEAUFORT, L. 1 E.

EVEL. I do conjure thee on thine honor, Vyvyan,
Hath he not—

VYV.   What ? (R. C.)

EVEL.   Forced quarrel on thee ? (C.)

VYV.   Quarrel
That were beyond his power.   Upon mine honor,
No, and thrice no !

EVEL.   I scarce dare yet believe thee.
VYV. Why then, I thus defy thee still to tremble.
      Away this weapon. (*throwing sword off* R. 1 E.) If I meet thy
          cousin,
      Both must be safe, for one will be unarmed.
EVEL. Mine own frank hero-lover, pardon me ;
      Yet need st thou not——
VYV.   Oh, as against the Spaniard,
      There will be swords enow in Vyvyan's war-ship—
      But' art thou sure his heart is touched so lightly ?
EVEL. Jealous, and now !
VYV.   No, the fair boy, 'tis pity !

Enter MARSDEN, L. 2 E.,

MARS.* My lady, sir, invites you to her presence ;
      Pray you this way.
EVEL.   Remember—O, remember,
      One word again, before we part ; but one !
VYV. One word.   Heaven make it joyous.
EVEL.   Joyous !
VYV. Soft, let me take that echo from thy lips
      As a good omen.   How my loud heart beats ! (*aside.*)
      Friend, to your lady. [*Exeunt* VYVYAN *and* MARSDEN, L. 1 E.
EVEL.   Gone !   The twilight world
      Hath its stars still—but mine ! Ah, woe is me !
                              [*Exit* EVELINE, L. 1 E.
SIR G. Why take the challenge, yet cast off the weapon ?
      Perchance, if, gentle, he forbears the boy ;
      "Perchance, if worldly wise, he fears the noble ;
      Or hath he, in his absence, chanced with Alton ?
      It matters not.   Like some dark necromancer,
      I raise the storm, then rule it thro' the fiend !
      Where waits this man without a hope ?
WRECK. (*coming down* C.).   Save vengeance !
SIR G. Wert thou as near when Beaufort spoke with Vyvyan ?
WRECK. Shall I repeat what Vyvyan said to Beaufort ?
SIR G. Thou know'st——
WRECK.   I know, that to St. Kinian's Cliff
      Will come the man whose hand wrote " felon " here.
                              (*touches face.*)
SIR G. Mark, what I ask is harder than to strike ;
      'Tis to forbear—but 'tis revenge with safety.
      Let Vyvyan first meet Beaufort ; watch what pass,
      And if the boy, whose hand obeys all passion,
      Should slay thy foeman, and forestall thy vengeance,
      Upon thy life (thou know'st, of old, Grey Malpas)
      Prevent not, nor assist.
WRECK.   That boy slay Vyvyan !
SIR G. For Vyvyan is unarmed.
WRECK.   Law calls that—murder !
SIR G. Which by thy witness, not unbacked by proof,
      Would give the murderer to the headsman's axe,
      And leave Grey Malpas heir of Montreville,
      And thee the richest squire in all his train.

---

*VYVYAN.   EVEL.   MARSDEN.   SIR GREY.
                   C.   .   L., *up.*

WRECK. I do conceive the scheme.   But if the youth
  Fail or relent——
SIR G.   I balk not thy revenge.
  And, if the corpse of Beaufort's rival be
  Found on the spot where armed Beaufort met him,
  To whom would justice track the death blow ?—Beaufort!
WRECK. No further words.   Or his, or mine the hand,
  Count one life less on earth ; and weave thy scheme—
  As doth the worm its coils—around the dead.
       [*Exit* WRECKLYFFE, D. *in* 3 G. *flat.*
SIR G. " One death avails as three, since for the mother
  Conscience and shame were sharper than the steel."
  So, I o'erleap the gulf, nor gaze below.
  On this side, desolate ruin ; bread begrudged ;
  And ribald scorn on impotent gray hairs ;
  The base poor cousin Boyhood threats with famine—
  Whose very dog is butchered if it bark :—
  On that side bended knees and fawning smiles,
  Ho ! ho ! there—Room for my lord's knights and pages !
  Room at the Court—room there, beside the throne !
  Ah, the new Earl of Montreville !   His lands
 . Cover two shires.   Such man should rule the state—
  A gracious lord—the envious call him old ;
  Not so—the coronet conceals gray hairs.
  He limp'd, they say, when he wore hose of serge.
  Tut, the slow march becomes the robes of ermine.
  Back, conscience, back !   Go scowl on boors and beggars—
  Room, smiling flatterers, room for the new Earl !
     —*(comes down front, proudly, as falls the)*

CURTAIN.

ACT IV.

SCENE I.—*Same as Scene I., Act II.*

Discover LADY MONTREVILLE, R. *Enter* VYVYAN, L.

LADY M. Thou com'st already to demand thy bride ?
VYV. Alas ! such nuptials are deferred.   This night
  The invader summons me—my sole bride, Honor,
  And my sole altar—England ! (*aside*) How to break it ?
LADY M. My Clarence on the land, and thou on sea,
  Both for their country armed !   Heaven shield ye both !
VYV. Say you that ?   *Both* ?—You who so love your son ?
LADY M. Better than life, I love him !
VYV. (*aside*).   I must rush
  Into the thick.   Time goads me ! (*aloud*) Had you not
  Another son ?   A first born ?
LADY M.   Sir !
VYV.   A son,
  On whom those eyes dwelt first—whose infant cry
  Broke first on that divine and holiest chord

In the deep heart of woman, which awakes
All Nature's tenderest music ?   Turn not from me
I know the mystery of thy mournful life.
Will it displease thee—will it—to believe
That son is living still ?

LADY M.   Sir—sir—such license
Expels your listener. (*turns* R.)

VYV.   No, thou wilt not leave me ?
I say, thou wilt not leave me—on my knees
I say, thou *shalt* not leave me !

LADY M.   Loose thine hold !

VYV. *I* am thy son—thine Edmond—thine own child !
Saved from the steel, the deep, the storm, the battle;
Rising from death to thee—the source of life !
Flung by kind Heaven once more upon thy breast,
Kissing thy robe, and clinging to thy knees.
Dost thou reject thy son ?

LADY M.   I have no son,
Save Clarence Beaufort.

VYV.   Do not—do not hear her,
Thou who, enthroned amid the pomp of stars,
Dost take no holier name than that of Father !
Thou hast no other son ?   O, cruel one !
Look—look—these letters to the priest who reared him—
See where thou call'st him " Edmond "—" child "—" life's all ! "
Can the words be so fresh on this frail record,
Yet fade, obliterate from the undying soul ?
By these—by these—by all the solemn past,
By thy youth's lover—by his secret grave,
By every kiss upon thine infant's cheek—
By every tear that wept his fancied death—
Grieve not that still a first-born calls thee " mother !

LADY M. Rise.   If these prove that such a son once lived,
Where are your proofs that still he lives in you ?

VYV. There ! in thine heart !—thine eyes that dare not face me !
Thy trembling limbs, each power, each pulse of being,
That vibrates at my voice !   Let pride encase thee
With nine-fold adamant, it rends asunder
At the great spell of Nature—Nature calls
Parent, come forth !

LADY M. (*aside*) Resolve gives way !   Lost Clarence !
What ! " Fall as Romans fell, on their swords' point ? "
No, Clarence, no ! (*turning fiercely*) Imposter ! If thy craft
Hath, by suborning most unworthy spies,
Sought in the ruins of a mourner's life
Some base whereon to pile this labored falsehood,
Let law laugh down the fable—Quit my presence.

VYV. No. I will not.

LADY M.   Will not ! Ho !

VYV.   Call your hirelings,
And let them hear me. (*to* R. C.) Lo, beneath thy roof,
And on the sacred hearth of sires to both,
Under their 'scutcheon, and before their forms
Which from the ghostly canvas I invoke
To hail their son—I take my dauntless stand,
Armed with my rights ; now bid your menials thrust
From his own hearth the heir of Montreville !

Enter SERVANTS, L.

LADY M. Seize on—— (*clasping her hands before her face.*)
         Out—out! (*aside*) His father stands before me
  In the son's image   No. I dare not!
FIRST SERVANT   Madam,
  Did you not summon us?
VYV.   They wait your mandate,
  Lady of Montreville.
LADY M.   I called not. Go!
                         [*Exeunt* SERVANTS, L.
  Art thou my son?   If so, have mercy, Edmond!
  Let Heaven attest with what remorseful soul
  I yielded to my ruthless father's will,
  And with cold lips profaned a second vow.
  I *had* a child—I was a parent true;
  But exiled from the parent's paradise.
  Not mine the frank joy in the face of day,
  The pride, the boast, the triumph, and the rapture;
  Thy couch was sought as with a felon's step,
  And whispering nature shuddered at detection.
  Ah, could'st thou guess what hell to loftier minds
  It is to live in one eternal lie
  Yet, spite of all, how dear thou wert!
VYV.   I was?
  Is the time past forever?   What my sin?
LADY M. I loved thee till another son was born,
  A blossom 'mid the snows.   Thou wert afar,
  Seen rarely—alien—on a stranger's breast
  Leaning for life. (*with great feeling*) But *this* thrice-blessed one
  Smiled in mine eyes, took being from my breast,
  Slept in mine arms; *here* love asked no concealment—
  Here the tear shamed not—*here* the kiss was glory—
  Here I put on my royalty of woman—
  The guardian, the protector; food, health, life—
  It clung to me for all.   Mother and child,
  Each was the all to each.
VYV.   O, prodigal,
  Such wealth to him, yet naught to spare to me!
LADY M. My boy grew up, my Clarence. Looking on him
  Men prized his mother more—so fair and stately,
  And the world deemed to such high state the heir!
  Years went; they told me that by Nature's death
  Thou hadst in boyhood passed away to heaven.
  I wept thy fate; and long ere tears were dried,
  The thought that danger, too, expired for Clarence,
  Did make thy memory gentle.
VYV.   Do you wish
  That I were still what once you wept to deem me?
LADY M. I did rejoice when my lip kissed thy brow;
  I did rejoice to give thy heart its bride;
  I would have drained my coffers for her dowry;
  But wouldst thou ask me if I can rejoice
  That a life rises from the grave abrupt
  To doom the life I cradled, reared, and wrapt
  From every breeze, to desolation?—No!

Vyv. What would you have me do ?

LADY M.   Accept the dowry,
And, blest with Eveline's love, renounce thy mother.

Vyv Renounce thee ! No—*these* lips belie not Nature !
Never !

LADY M.   Enough—I can be mean no more,
E'en in the prayer that asked his life. Go, slay it.

Vyv. Why must my life slay his ?

LADY M.   Since his was shaped
To soar to power—not grovel to dependence—
And I do seal his death-writ when I say,
" Down to the dust, Usurper ; bow the knee
And sue for alms to the true Lord of Beaufort."
Those words shall not be said—I'll find some nobler. ,
Thy rights are clear. The law might long defer them—
I do forestall the law. These lands be thine.
Wait not my death to lord it in my hall :
Thus I say not to Clarence, " Be dependent "—
But I *can* say, " Share poverty with me."
I go to seek him ; at his side depart ;
He spurns thine alms : I wronged thee—take thy vengeance !

Vyv. Merciless—hold, and hear me—I—alms !—vengeance !—
True—true, this heart a mother never cradled,
Or she had known it better.

LADY M.   Edmond !

Vyv.   Hush !
Call me that name no more—it dies forever !
Nay, I renounce thee not, for that were treason
On the child s lip. Parent, renounce—thy—child !
As for these nothings, (*giving papers*) take them ; if you dread
To find words, once too fond, they're blurr'd already—
You'll see but tears : tears of such sweetness, madam.
I did not think of lands and halls, pale Countess,
I did but think—these arms shall clasp a mother.
" Now they are worthless—take them. Never guess
How covetous I was—how hearts, cast off,
Pine for their rights—rights not of parchment, lady."
Part we, then, thus ? No, put thine arms around me ;
Let me remember in the years to come,
That I have lived to say, a mother blessed me ! (*kneels.*)

LADY M. Oh, Edmond, Edmond, thou hast conquered !
Thy father's voice !—his eyes ! Look down from heaven,
Bridegroom, and pardon me ; I bless thy child !

Vyv. Hark ! she has blessed her son ! It mounts to heaven,
The blessing of the mother on her child !
Mother, and mother ;—how the word thrills thro' me !
Mother again, dear mother ! Place thy hand
Here—on my heart. Now thou hast felt it beat,
Wilt thou misjudge it more ?

LADY M.   Oh !

Vyv.   Recoil'st thou still ?

LADY M. (*breaking from him*). What have I done ?—betrayed, condemned my Clarence ! (*to n., frantically.*)

Vyv. (c.). Condemned thy Clarence ! By thy blessing, No !
That blessing was my birthright. I have won
That which I claimed. Give Clarence all the rest.
Silent, as sacred, be the memory

Of this atoning honr.   Look, evermore (*kissing her*)
Thus—thus I seal the secret of thy first-born !
Now, only Clarence lives !   Heaven guard thy Clarence !
Now deem me dead to thee.   Farewell, farewell !

[*Exit* VYVYAN, L.

LADY M. (*rushing after him*). Hold, hold—too generous, hold ! Come
back, my son !   [*Exit* LADY MONTREVILLE, L.

Scene changes to

SCENE II.—*Sea and Rocks in 4th grooves.*

Enter LORD BEAUFORT, L. 1 E.

LORD B. And still not here !   The hour has long since passed.
I'll climb yon tallest peak, and strain mine eyes
Down the sole path between the cliff and ocean.
                    (*goes up steps* R., *and off* R. 2 E.)

Enter WRECKLYFFE, L. 1 E.

WRECK. The boors first grinned, then paled, and crept away ;
The tavern-keeper slunk, and muttered " Hangdog ! "
And the she-drudge whose rough hand served the drink,
Stifled her shriek, and let the tankard fall !
It was not so in the old merry days :
Then the scarred hangdog was " fair gentleman."
And—but the reckoning waits.   Why tarries he ? (*beat on bass
    drum, with diminuendo beats, for signal gun, and its echoes.*)
A signal !   Ha !

VYV. (*off* L.)   I come, I come !

WRECK. (*grasping his cutlass, but receding as he sees* BEAUFORT *enter
R. 1 E.*)   Hot lordling !
I had well night forestalled thee.   Patience !
                    [*Exit around set rock*, L. C.

LORD B. (R. 2 E., *on platform.*)   Good !
From crag to crag he bounds—my doubts belied him ;
His haste is eager as my own.

Enter VYVYAN, L. 1 E., *crossing and going up* R. *steps.*

                              Sir, welcome.
                    (*both on first platform*, R. U. E.)

VYV. Stay me not, stay me not !   Thou hast all else
But honor—rob me not of that !   Unhand me !

LORD B. Unhand thee ? yes—to take thy ground and draw.

VYV. Thou know'st not what thou sayest.   Let me go !

LORD B. Thyself didst name the place and hour :

VYV.   For here
I thought to clasp—(*aside*) I have no brother now !

LORD B. He thought to clasp his Eveline.   Death and madness !

VYV. Eveline !   Thou lov'st not Eveline.   " Be consoled.
Thou hast not known affliction—hast not stood
Without the porch of the sweet home of men ;
Thou hast leaned upon no reed that pierced the heart ;
Thou hast not known what it is, when in the desert

The hopeless find the fountain." Happy boy,
Thou hast not loved. Leave love to man and sorrow!
LORD B. Dost thou presume upon my years? Dull scoffer!
The brave is man betimes—the coward never.
Boy if I be, my playmates have been veterans;
My toy a sword, and my first lesson valor.
And, had I taken challenge as thou hast,
And on the ground replied to bold defiance
With random words implying dastard taunts,
" With folded arms, pale lip, and haggard brow,"
I'd never live to call myself a man.
Thus says the boy, since manhood is so sluggard,
Soldier and captain. Do not let me strike thee!
VYV. Do it,—and tell thy mother, when thy hand
Outraged my cheek, I pardoned thee, and pitied.
LORD B. Measureless insult! Pitied! (*drum for gun as before.*)
VYV.   There again!
And still so far! Out of my path, insane one!
Were there naught else, thy youth, thy mother's love
Should make thee sacred to a warrior's arm—
Out of my path. Thus, then. (*suddenly lifts, and puts him aside.*)
           Oh, England—England!
Do not reject me too!—I come! I come!
           (*up the steps to upper platform.*)
LORD B. Thrust from his pathway—every vein runs fire!
Thou shalt not thus escape me—Stand or die!
    (*sword in hand, drives* VYVYAN *to the edge of the cliff, and he grasps, for support, the bough of tree.*)
VYV. Forbear, forbear!
LORD B.   Thy blood on thine own head! (*drum for gun as before. As* BEAUFORT *lifts his sword and strikes,* VYVYAN *retreats—the bough breaks, and* VYVYAN *swings* L., *and down into centre trap.*)
WRECK. (*rises* R. C. *by trap*). Is the deed done? If not, this steel completes it. (*waves cutlass and exit down trap.* LORD BEAUFORT *sinks on his knee in horror. Work ship on* R. *to* L., *across.*)

SLOW CURTAIN.

———

ACT V.

SCENE I.—*Same as Act IV., Scene II.*

Enter SIR GREY DE MALPAS, L., *leaning on cane.*

SIR G. A year—and Wrecklyffe still is mute and absent,
Even as Vyvyan is! Most clear! He saw,
And haply shared, the murderous deed of Beaufort;
And Beaufort's wealth hath bribed him to desert
Penury and me. That Clarence slew his brother
I cannot doubt. He shuts me from his presence;
But I have watched him, wandering, lone, yet haunted—

Marked the white lip and glassy eyes of one
For whom the grave has ghosts, and silence, horror.
His mother, on vague pretext of mistrust
That I did sell her first-born to the pirate.
Excludes me from her sight, but sends me alms
Lest the world cry, " See, her poor cousin starves ! "
Can she guess Beaufort's guilt ? Nay ! For she lives !
I know that deed, which, told unto the world,
Would make me heir of Montreville. O, mockery !
For how proceed ?—no proof ! How charge ?—no witness !
How cry, " Lo ! murder! " yet produce no corpse !

Enter ALTON, R.

ALTON. Sir Grey de Malpas ! I was on my way
    To your own house.
SIR G.   Good Alton—can I serve you ?
ALTON. The boy I took from thee, returned a man
    Twelve months ago : mine oath absolved.
SIR G.   'Tis true.
ALTON. Here did I hail the rightful lord of Montreville,
    And from these arms he rushed to claim his birthright.
SIR G. (*aside*). She never told me this.
ALTON.   That night his war-ship
    Sailed to our fleet. I deemed him with the battle.
    Time went ; Heaven's breath had scattered the Armada.
    I sate at my porch to welcome him—he came not
    I said, " His mother has abjured her offspring,
    And law detains him while he arms for justice."
    Hope sustained patience till to-day.
SIR G.   To-day ?
ALTON. The very friend who had led me to his breast
    Returns, and——
SIR G. (*soothingly.*) Well ?
ALTON.   He fought not with his country.
SIR G. And this cold friend lets question sleep a year ?
ALTON. His bark too rashly chased the flying foe ;
    Was wrecked on hostile shores ; and he a prisoner.
SIR G. Lean on my arm, thou'rt faint.
ALTON.   Oh, Grey de Malpas,
    Can men so vanish—save in murderous graves ?
    You turn away.
SIR G.   What murder without motive ?
    And who had motive here ?
ALTON.   Unnatural kindred.
SIR G. Kindred ! Ensnare me not ! Mine, too, that kindred.
    Old man, beware how thou asperse (*pause*) Lord Beaufort !
ALTON. Beaufort ! Oh, horror ! How the instinctive truth
    Starts from thy lips !
SIR G.   From mine ?
ALTON.   Yes. Not of man
    Ask pardon, if accomplice——
SIR G.   I, accomplice !
    Nay, since 'tis my good name thou sulliest now—
    This is mine answer : Probe ; examine ; search ;
    And call on justice to belie thy slander.
    Go, seek the aid of stout Sir Godfrey Seymour ;

A dauntless magistrate ; strict, upright, honest ;
(*aside*). At heart a Puritan, and hates a Lord,
With other slides that fit into my grooves.

ALTON. He bears with all the righteous name thou giv'st him,
Thy zeal acquits thyself.

SIR G.   And charges none.

ALTON. Heaven reads the heart.   Man can but track the deed.
My task is stern.   [*Exit* ALTON, L.

SIR G.   Scent lies—suspicion dogs,
And with hot breath pants on the flight of conscience.
Ah ! who comes here ?   Sharp wit, round all occasion !

Enter FALKNER *with* SAILORS, L.

FALK. Learn all you can—when latest seen, and where—
Meanwhile I seek yon towers.   [*Exeunt* SAILORS, L.

SIR G.   Doubtless, fair sir,
I speak to Vyvyan's friend.   My name is Malpas—
Can it be true, as Alton doth inform me,
That you suspect your comrade died by murder ?

FALK. Murder !

SIR G.   And by a rival's hand ?   Amazed !
Yet surely so I did conceive the priest.

FALK. Murder !—a rival !—true, he loved a maiden !

SIR G. In yonder halls !

FALK.   Despair !   Am I too late
For all but vengeance !   Speak, sir—who this rival ?

SIR G. Vengeance !—fie—seek those towers, and learn compassion.
Sad change indeed, since here, at silent night,
Your Vyvyan met the challenge of Lord Beaufort.

FALK. A challenge ?—here ?—at night ?

SIR G.   Yes, this the place.
How sheer the edge ! crag, cave, and chasm below !
If the foot slipped,—nay, let us think slipped heedless,—
Or some weak wounded man were headlong plunged,
What burial place more secret ?

FALK.   Hither, look !
Look where, far down the horrible descent,
Through some fresh cleft rush subterranean waves,
How wheel and circle ghastly swooping wings !

SIR G. The sea-gulls ere a storm,

FALK.   No !   Heaven is clear !
The storm *they* tell, speeds lightning towards the guilty.
So have I seen the foul birds in lone creeks
Sporting around the shipwrecked seaman's bones.
Guide me, ye spectral harbingers ! (*down* C *trap.   Music.*)

SIR G.   From bough
To bough he swings—from peak to slippery peak
I see him dwindling down ;—the loose stones rattle ;
He falls—he falls—but 'lights on yonder ledge,
And from the glaring sun turns steadfast eyes
Where still the sea-gulls wheel ; now crawls, now leaps ;
Crags close around him—not a glimpse nor sound !
O, diver for the dead ! (*sinks down as if watching* FALKNER ;
    then rises) Bring up but bones,
And round the skull I'll wreathe my coronet.   [*Exit*, R.

Scene changes to

SCENE II.—*Interior in 1st grooves.*

Enter LADY MONTREVILLE *and* MARSDEN, L.

LADY M. Will he nor hunt nor hawk?   This constant gloom!
   Canst thou not guess the cause?   He *was* so joyous!
MARS. Young plants need air and sun; man's youth the world.
   Young men should pine for action.   Comfort, madam,
   The cause is clear, if you recall the date.
LADY M. Thou hast marked the date?
MARS.   Since that bold seaman's visit.
LADY M. Thy tongue runs riot, man.   How should that stranger—
   I say a stranger, strike dismay in Beaufort?
MARS. Dismay!   Not that, but emulation!
LADY M.   Ay!
   You speak my thoughts, and I have prayed our Queen
   To rank your young lord with her chivalry;
   This day mine envoy should return.
MARS.   This day?
   Let me ride forth and meet him!
LADY M.   Go!   [*Exit* MARSDEN, L.
                                      'Tis true!
   Such was the date.   Hath Clarence guessed the secret—
   Guessed that a first-born lives?   I dread to question!
   Yet sure the wronged was faithful, and the wrong
   Is my heart's canker-worm and gnaws unseen.
   Where wanderest thou, sad Edmond?   Not one word
   To say thou liv'st—thy very bride forsaken,
   As if love, frozen at the parent well-spring,
   Left every channel dry!   What hollow tread,
   Heavy and weary falls?   Is that the step
   Which touched the mean earth with a lightsome scorn,
   As if the air its element?

Enter, BEAUFORT, R., *in mantle.*

LORD B.   Cold! cold!
   And yet I saw the beggar doff his frieze,
   Warm in his rags.   I shiver under ermine.
   For me 'tis never summer—never—never!
LADY M. How fares my precious one?
LORD B.   Well;—but so cold.
   Ho! there! without!

Enter SERVANT, L.

                  Wine! wine!   [*Exit* SERVANT, L.
LADY M.   Alas! alas!
   Why, this is fever—thy hand burns.
LORD B.   That hand!
   Ay, *that* hand always burns.

Re-enter SERVANT, L., *with wine in goblet, on salver.*

                  Look you—the cup

The wondrous Tuscan jeweller, Cellini,
Made for a king! A king's gift to thy father!
What? Serve such gauds to me!

LADY M.   Thyself so ordered
In the proud whims thy light heart made so graceful.

LORD B. Was I proud once? Ha! ha! what's this?—not wine?

SERVANT. The Malvoisie your lordship's friends, last year,
Esteemed your rarest.

LORD B.   How one little year
Hath soured it into nausea! Faugh—'tis rank.

LADY M. (*to* SERVANT). Send for the leech—quick—go.
                    [*Exit* SERVANT, L.
                         Oh, Clarence! Clarence!
Is this the body's sickness, or the soul's?
Is it life's youngest sorrow, love misplaced?
Thou dost not still love Eveline?

LORD B.   Did I love her?

LADY M. Or one whose birth might more offend my pride?
Well, I *am* proud. But I would hail as daughter
The meanest maiden from whose smile thy lip
Caught smiles again. Thy smile is day to me.

LORD B. Poor mother, fear not. Never hermit-monk,
Gazing on skulls in lone sepulchral cells,
Had heart as proof to woman's smile as mine.

LADY M. The court—the camp—ambition——

Enter MARSDEN, *with a letter*, R.

MARS.   From the Queen!
(*while the* COUNTESS *reads*, MARSDEN, *turning to* LORD BEAUFORT)
My dear young lord, be gay! The noblest knight,
In all the land, Lord Essex, on his road
From conquered Cadiz, "with the armed suite
That won his laurels," sends before to greet you,
And prays you will receive him in your halls.

LORD B. The flower of England's gentry, spotless Essex!
Sully him not, old man, bid him pass on.

LADY M. Joy, Beaufort, joy! August Elizabeth
Owns thee her knight, and bids thee wear her colors,
And break thy maiden lance for England's lady.

LORD B. I will not go. Barbed steeds and knightly banners—
Baubles and gewgaws!

MARS.   Glorious to the young.

LORD B. Ay—to the young! Oh, when did poet dreams
Ever shape forth such a fairy land as youth!
Gossamer hopes, pearled with the dews of morn,
Gay valor, bounding light on welcome peril,—
Errors themselves, the sparkling overflow,
Of life as headlong, but as pure as streams
That rush from sunniest hill-tops kissing heaven,—
Lo! *that* is youth. Look on my soul, old man,
Well—is it not more gray than those blanched hairs? (*falls in
seat*, c.)

LADY M. He raves. Heed not his words. Go speed the leech!
                    [*Exit* MARSDEN, R., *quickly*.
(*aside*). I know these signs—by mine own soul I know them;
This is nor love, nor honor's sigh for action,

Nor Nature's milder suffering. This is guilt!
Clarence—now, side by side, I sit with thee!
Put thine arms round me, lean upon my breast—
It is a mother's breast. So, that is well;
Now—whisper low—what is thy crime?

LORD B. (*bursting into tears*).   Oh, mother!
Would thou hadst never borne me!

LADY M.   Ah, ungrateful!

LORD B. No—for thy sake I speak. Thou—justly proud,
For thou art pure; thou, on whose whitest name
Detraction spies no soil—dost thou say "crime"
Unto thy son; and is his answer tears?

Enter EVELINE, R., *weaving flowers as in Act I.*

EVEL.   Blossoms, I weave ye
        To drift on the sea,
      Say when ye find him
        Who sang " Woe is me!"
(*approaching* BEAUFORT) Have you no news?

LORD B.   Of whom?

EVEL.   Of Vyvyan?

LORD B. That name! Her reason wanders; and oh, mother,
When that name's uttered—so doth mine—hush, hush it.
(EVELINE *goes to window, and throws garland through*)

LADY M. Kill me at once—or when I ask again,
What is thy crime?—reply, "No harm to Vyvyan!"

LORD B. (*breaking away*). Unhand me! Let me go!
           [*Exit* LORD BEAUFORT, L., *wildly.*

LADY M.   This pulse beats still!
Nature rejects me!

EVEL.   Come, come—see the garland,
It dances on the waves so merrily.

Enter MARSDEN, R.

MARS. (*drawing aside* LADY M.). Forgive this haste. Amid St. Kini-
    an's Cliffs
Where, once an age, on glassy peaks may glide
The shadow of a man, a stranger venturing
Hath found bleached human bones, and to your hall,
Nearest at hand, and ever famed for justice,
Leads on the crowd, and saith the dead was Vyvyan.

EVEL. Ha! who named Vyvyan? Has he then come back?

MARS. Fair mistress, no.

LADY M.   If on this terrible earth
Pity lives still—lead her away. Be tender.

EVEL, (*approaching* LADY M.). I promised him to love you as a mo-
    ther.
Kiss me, and trust in Heaven! He will return!
           [*Exeunt* EVELINE *and* MARSDEN.

LADY M. These horrors are unreal.

Enter SERVANT, R.

SERVANT.   Noble mistress.

Sir Godfrey Seymour, summoned here in haste,
Craves your high presence in the Justice Hall.

LADY M. Mine—mine ?   Where goest thou ?

SERVANT.   Sir Godfrey bade me
Seek my young lord.

LADY M.   Stir not.   My son is ill.
Thyself canst witness how the fever—(*hurrying* R.) Marsden !

Enter MARSDEN, R.

My stricken Clarence !—In his state, a rumor
Of—of what passes here, might blast life—reason :
Go, lure him hence—if he resist, use force
As to a maniac.   Ah ! good old man, thou lov'st him ;
His innocent childhood played around thy knees—
I know I can trust *thee*—Quick—speak not :—Save !
                              [*Exit* MARSDEN, L.

(*to* SERVANT) Announce my coming.   [*Exit* SERVANT, R.
                         This day, life to shield
The living son :—Death, with the dead, to-morrow !
                         [*Exit* LADY MONTREVILLE, R.

SCENE III.—*Castle Hall, in 5th grooves.*

Discover SIR GODFREY SEYMOUR *seated,* L.   CLERK, *at table, employed in
writing.*   SIR GREY DE MALPAS *standing up* L., *near* SIR GODFREY.
FALKNER, L. C.   HALBERDIERS, SERVANTS.

SIR GODF. (*to* FALKNER). Be patient, sir, and give us ampler proof
To deem yon undistinguishable bones
The relics of your friend.

FALK.   That gentleman
Can back my oath, that these, the plume, the gem
Which Vyvyan wore—I found them on the cliff.

SIR GODF. Verily, is it so ?

SIR G. (*with assumed reluctance*). Sith law compel me—
Yes, I must vouch it.

Enter SERVANT, R. 2 E.

SERVANT (*placing a chair of state*). Sir, my lady comes.

SIR G.   And her son.

Enter, R. 2 E., LADY MONTREVILLE, *and seats herself,* R. C.

SIR GODF. You pardon, madam, mine imperious duties,
And know my dismal task——

LADY M.   Pray you be brief, sir.

SIR GODF. Was, this time year, the captain of a war-ship,
Vyvyan his name, your guest ?

LADY M.   But one short day—
To see my ward, whom he had saved from pirates.

SIR GODF. I pray you, madam, in his converse with you
Spoke he of any foe, concealed or open,
Whom he had cause to fear ?

LADY M.   Of none !

SIR GODF.   Nor know you
Of any such ?

LADY M. (*after a pause*). I do not.
SIR GODF. (*aside to* FALKNER).   Would you farther
        Question this lady, sir ?
FALK.   No, she is a woman,
        And mother; let her go.   I wait Lord Beaufort.
SIR GODF. Madam, no longer will we task your presence.

Enter LORD BEAUFORT, D. *in* F., *breaking from* MARSDEN, *and other* AT-
                TENDANTS.

LORD B. Off, dotard, off!   Guests in our hall!
LADY M.   He is ill.
        Sore ill—fierce fever—I will lead him forth.
        Come, Clarence; darling come !
LORD B.   Who is this man ?
FALK. The friend of Vyvyan, whose pale bones plead yonder.
LORD B. I—I will go.   Let's steal away, my mother.
FALK. Lost friend, in war, how oft thy word was " Spare."—
        Methinks I hear thee now.   (*draws* LORD BEAUFORT *to* R. C.)
                        Young lord, I came
        Into these halls, demanding blood for blood—
        But thy remorse (this *is* remorse) disarms me.
        Speak; do but say—(look, I am young myself,
        And know how hot is youth ;) speak—do but say,
        After warm words, struck out from jealous frenzy,
        Quick swords were drawn: Man's open strife with man—
        Passion, not murder : Say this, and may law
        Pardon thee, as a soldier does !
SIR GREY (*to* MARSDEN).   Call Eveline,
        She can attest our young lord's innocence.   [*Exit* MARSDEN.
FALK. He will not speak, sir, let my charge proceed.
LADY M. (*aside*). Whate'er the truth—of that—of that hereafter,
        Now but remember, child, thy birth, thy name ;—
        Thy mother's heart, it beats beside thee—take
        Strength from its pulses.
LORD B.   Keep close, and for thy sake
        I will not cry—" 'Twas passion, yet still, murder ! "
SIR GODF. (*who has been conversing aside with* SIR GREY). Then jealous
            love the motive ?   Likelier that
        Than Alton's wilder story.

            Enter EVELINE *and* MARSDEN.

                        Sweet young madam,
        If I be blunt, forgive me ; we are met
        On solemn matters which relate to one
        Who, it is said, was your betrothed :
EVEL.   To Vyvyan !
SIR GODF. 'Tis also said, Lord Beaufort crossed his suit,
        And your betrother resented.
EVEL.   No ! forgave.
SIR G. Yes, when you feared some challenge from Lord Beaufort,
        Did Vyvyan not cast down his sword and say,
        " Both will be safe, for one will be unarmed ? (*great sensation
            through the hall.*)
FALKNER *and* SIR GODFREY. Unarmed !
EVEL.   His very words !

FALK. Oh, vile assassin!

SIR GODF. Accuser, peace! This is most grave. Lord Beaufort,
Upon such tokens, with your own strange bearing,
As ask appeal to more august tribunal,
You stand accused of purposed felon murder
On one named Vyvyan, Captain of the *Dreadnaught*—
"Wouldst thou say aught against this solemn charge?"

EVEL. Murdered!—he—Vyvyan! Thou his murderer, Clarence,
In whose rash heat my hero loved frank valor?
Lo! I, to whom his life is as the sun
Is to the world—with my calm trust in Heaven
Mantle thee thus. Now, speak!

LADY M. (*aside*). Be firm—deny, and live.

LORD B. (*attempting to be haughty*). You call my bearing "strange?"
—what marvel, sir?
Stunned by such charges, of a crime so dread.
What proof against me? (SIR GREY *meets* ALTON *up* R. *and keeps him in talk.*)

LADY M. Words deposed by whom?
A man unknown;—a girl's vague fear of quarrel—
His motive what? A jealous anger! Phantoms!
Is not my son mine all! And yet this maid
I plighted to another. Had I done so
If loved by him, and at the risk of life?
Again, I ask all present what the motive?

ALTON. (*comes down with* SIR GREY).* Rank, fortune, birthright.
Miserable woman!

LADY M. Whence com'st thou, pale accuser?

ALTON. From the dead!
Which of ye two will take the post I leave?
Which of ye two will draw aside that veil,
Look on the bones behind, and cry, "I'm guiltless?"
Hast thou conspired with him to slay thy first-born,
Or knows he not that Vyvyan was his brother? (LADY MONTRE-
VILLE *swoons.* EVELINE *rushes to* LADY MONTREVILLE.)

LORD B. My brother! No, no, no! (*clutching hold of* SIR GREY.) Kinsman, he lies!

SIR G. Alas! (R. *front.*)

LORD B. Wake, mother wake. I ask not speech.
Lift but thy brow—one flash of thy proud eye
Would strike these liars dumb!

ALTON. Read but those looks
To learn that thou art——

LORD B. Cain! (*grasping* FALKNER). Out with thy sword—(L.)
Hew off this hand. Thou calledst me "assassin!"
Too mild—say "fratricide!" Cain, Cain, thy brother! (*falls sobbing,* C. *front*)

EVEL. It cannot be so! No. Thou wondrous Mercy,
That, from the pirate's knife, the funeral seas
And all their shapes of death, didst save the lone one,
To prove to earth how vainly man despairs
While God is in the heavens—I cling to thee,
As Faith unto its anchor! (*to* SIR GREY) Back, false kinsman!
I tell thee Vyvyan lives—the boy is guiltless!

*EVEL.   LADY M.   BEAUF.   ALTON.   SIR GREY.   SIR GODFREY.
R.   R. C.   C.   L. C.   L.

" FALK. Poor, noble maid ! How my heart bleeds for her ! "

LADY M. (*starting up*). Sentence us both ! or stay,—would law con-
    demn
    A child so young, if I had urged him to it ?

SIR GODF. Unnatural mother, hush ! Sir Grey, to you,
    Perchance ere long, by lives too justly forfeit,
    Raised to this earldom, I entrust these—prisoners. (*motions to*
    HALBERDIERS, *who advance to arrest* BEAUFORT, *who rises,*
    and LADY MONTREVILLE.)

MARS. Oh, day of woe !

SIR G.   Woe—yes ! Make way for us. (*trumpet.*)

            Enter SERVANT, D. *in* F.

SEAVANT. My lord of Essex just hath passed the gates ;
    But an armed knight who rode beside the Earl,
    After brief question to the crowd without,
    Sprang from his steed, and forces here his way ! (*trumpet*
    flourish.)

    Enter VYVYAN, *in armor, his vizor three-parts down.*

VYV. Forgiveness of all present !

SIR GODF.   Who art thou ?

VYV. A soldier, knighted by the hand of Essex
    Upon the breach of Cadiz.

SIR GODF.   What thy business ?

VYV. To speak the truth. Who is the man accused
    Of Vyvyan's murder ?

SIR G.   You behold him yonder.

VYV. 'Tis false.

SIR G. (R. *front*). His own lips have confessed his crime.

VYV. (*throwing down his gauntlet, to* R.). This to the man whose crush-
    ing lie bows down
    Upon the mother's bosom that young head !
    Say you " confess'd ! " Oh, tender, tender conscience !
    Vyvyan, rough sailor, galled him and provoked ;
    He raised his hand. To the sharp verge of the cliff
    Vyvyan recoiled, backed by an outstretched bough,
    The bough gave way—he fell, but not to perish ;
    Saved by a bush-grown ledge that broke his fall ;
    Long stunned he lay ; when opening dizzy eyes,
    On a gray crag between him and the abyss
    He saw the face of an old pirate foe ;
    Saw the steel lifted, saw it flash and vanish,
    As a dark mass rushed thro' the moonlit air
    Dumb into deeps below—the indignant soil
    Had slid like glass beneath the murderer's feet,
    And his own death-spring whirled him to his doom.
    Then Vyvyan rose, and, crawling down the rock,
    Stood by the foe, who, stung to late remorse
    By hastening death, gasped forth a dread confession.
    The bones ye find are those of Murder's agent—
    Murder's arch-schemer—Who ? Ho ! Grey De Malpas,
    Stand forth ! Thou art the man !

SIR GREY.   Hemm'd round with toils,

Soul, crouch no more !   Base hireling, doff thy mask,
And my sword writes the lie upon thy front.
By Beaufort's hand died Vyvyan—(*draws sword.*)

VYV.   As the spell
Shatters the sorcerer when his fiends desert him,
Let thine own words bring doom upon thyself !
Now face the front on which to write the lie. (*removes hemlet,*
taken away by PAGES.   SIR GREY *drops his sword and staggers*
back into the arms of MARSDEN *and* ALTON, R. *front.*)

EVEL. Thou liv'st, thou liv'st—(*removes white from her cheeks and shows*
the color.)

VYV. (*kneeling to her,* c.).   Is life worth something still ?

SIR GREY. Air, air—my staff—some chord seems broken here. (*press-*
ing his heart.)
Marsden, your lord shot his poor cousin's dog ;
In the dog's grave—mark !—bury the poor cousin. (*sinks ex-*
hausted, and is borne out, R. 2 E.)

VYV. Mine all on earth, if I may call thee mine.

EVEL. Thine, thine, thro' life, thro' death—one heart, one grave !
" I knew thou wouldst return, for I have lived
In thee so utterly, thou couldst not die
And I live still.—The dial needs the sun ;
But love reflects the image of the loved,
Tho' every beam be absent !—Thine, all thine ! "

LADY M. My place is forfeit on thy breast, not his. (*pointing to*
BEAUFORT.)
Clarence, embrace thy brother, and my first-born.
His rights are clear—my love for thee suppressed them—
He may forgive me yet—wilt *thou* ?

BEAU.   Forgive thee !
Oh mother, what is rank to him who hath stood
Banished from out the social pale of men,
Bowed like a slave, and trembling as a felon ?
Heaven gives me back mine ermine, innocence ;
And my lost dignity of manhood, honor.
I miss naught else.—Room there for me, my brother !

VYV. Mother, come first !—love is as large as heaven !

" FALK. But why so long——

VYV.   What ! could I face thee, friend,
Or claim my bride, till I had won back honor ?
The fleet had sailed—the foeman was defeated—
And on the earth I laid me down to die.
The prince of England's youth, frank-hearted Essex,
Passed by—— But later I will tell you how
Pity woke question ; soldier felt for soldier.
Essex then, nobly envying Drake's renown,
Conceived a scheme, kept secret till our clarions,
Startling the towers of Spain, told earth and time
How England answers the invader.   Clarence,"
Look brother—I have won the golden spurs of knighthood !
For worldly gifts, we'll share them—hush, my brother ;
Love me, and thy gift is as large as mine.
Fortune stints gold to some ; impartial Nature
Shames her in proffering more than gold to all—
Joy in the sunshine, beauty on the earth,
And love reflected in the glass of conscience ;
Are these so mean ?   Place grief and guilt beside them,

Decked in a sultan's splendor, and compare!
The world's most royal he-itage is his
Who most enjoys, most loves, and most forgives.

All form picture. Music.

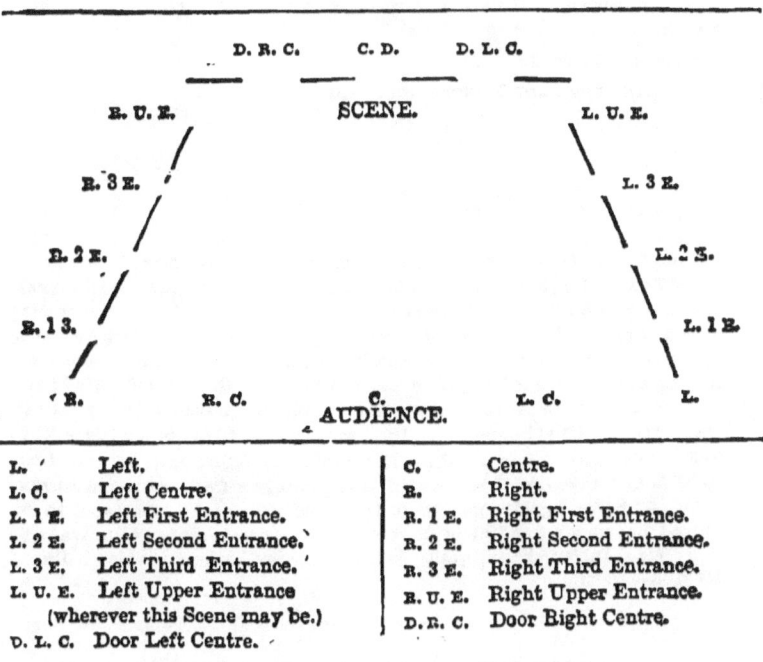

CURTAIN (*slow*).

EXPLANATION OF THE STAGE DIRECTIONS.

The Actor is supposed to face the Audience.

L.	Left.	C.	Centre.
L. C.	Left Centre.	R.	Right.
L. 1 E.	Left First Entrance.	R. 1 E.	Right First Entrance.
L. 2 E.	Left Second Entrance.	R. 2 E.	Right Second Entrance.
L. 3 E.	Left Third Entrance.	R. 3 E.	Right Third Entrance.
L. U. E.	Left Upper Entrance	R. U. E.	Right Upper Entrance.
	(wherever this Scene may be.)	D. R. C.	Door Right Centre.
D. L. C.	Door Left Centre.		

COSTUMES—Concluded.

SERVANT.—Gray livery, turned up with orange.

SAILORS.—In Guernsey shirts, with belts supporting cutlasses and pistols; high boots; jackets gathered in at the waist by sashes; tights and shoes.

SERVANTS.—Like first servant.

CLERK TO SEYMOUR.—In black.

HALBERDIERS.—Steel caps; back, breast and thigh plates; boots; halberds for them.

VILLAGERS.—As usual.

LADY MONTREVILLE.—Fair-haired; make up after portraits of Queen Elizabeth; if the ruff does not look becomingly, have a deep ruffled lace collar open in front; jewelled stomacher; bodice cut square at the bosom; with lace let in; velvet body and skirt, with deep border jewelled cross to long necklace; earrings; wedding-ring; velvet band, with jewelled beading, on the head, just behind the front puffs of the hair. *Act V.:* Dark velvet skirt and body; the bodice faced in the front with white lace, crossed with violet braid.

EVELINE.—Hair puffed in front, and in loose ringlets in a bunch at back of head; string of pearls three times around the neck, ending in locket and cross; blue body and skirt; skirt opens in front and shows white under-skirt; trimmed with gold cord. *Act V.:* White satin dress; face pale, with the white on the cheeks to come off and show color under, at a touch of hand dampened by a breath.

VILLAGE GIRLS.—As usual.

WAITING WOMEN FOR LADY MONTREVILLE.—As usual.

PROPERTIES, *(See Scenery).*

Act I.—Scene I.: Spade; coin for VYVYAN; weapons for sailors. *Scene II.:* A handful of flowers for EVELINE to enter with, ready R. 1 E.; cane for MALPAS. *Act II.—Scene I.:* Table and three chairs; on table a two-handled silver goblet; cups and plates of fruit for three. *Scene II.:* Four cannon in block carriages, not to be touched; a cresset or beacon basket, at end of a rod, hung out from R. 1 E.; sheet of printed paper, foolscap size. *Act III.—Scene I.:* Staff; roll of MSS. tied up, for ALTON. *Scene II.:* Sword hilt in sheath, for VYVYAN to throw aside. *Act IV.—Scene I.:* MSS. roll, as in Act III., Scene I., for VYVYAN to enter with, ready R. *Scene II.:* Profile miniature ship, to work from R. to L. U. E. line. *Act V.—Scene I.:* Canes, as before, for MALPAS and ALTON. *Scene II.:* Salver; gold cup, jewelled; letter, with sealed silk band, to be opened on stage; handful of flowers for EVELINE to enter with, ready R. *Scene III.:* Table; chairs; quills, inkdishes, paper, books, on table; halberds for Halberdiers.

TIME OF PLAYING—TWO HOURS AND FORTY-FIVE MINUTES.

NOTE.

The few "cuts" are marked by enclosure between quotations, as "———."